Motivated in Missouri
Book 28 in At the Altar
Kirsten Osbourne

Chapter One

Melanie Carter glanced up from the tray of diced carrots she was removing from the commercial freeze-dryer in her test kitchen as her friend and co-worker, Abigail Lindstrom walked in, hanging up her sweater and pulling on an apron and a baseball cap to keep her hair from getting into the food. "Hey! I just finished another round of carrots. I really want to use them in the split pea soup recipe we're working on today."

Abigail nodded. "I agree with that. And we're doing barley, right?"

"I think so. I think this is going to be a recipe I want to share on the website for Melanie's Meals, so people can make the mix themselves, but it would also be fun to produce it for people to buy in all the standard quantities of course."

"Are we doing meat in it? Or suggesting people add meat when they cook it?"

Melanie pursed her lips, thinking more about it. She'd been debating that particular thing for days. "I think we have enough protein in the other ingredients. If people feel like they want meat to go into it, they can add that themselves. I guess we could make one with TVP, but you know how I feel about soy." She shuddered delicately.

Abigail laughed. "Not everyone in the world is allergic to soy like you are, but I don't think it's healthy for anyone. We'll play with it and see what we think. And yes, I'll fall on the sword and try the ones with TVP." Texturized vegetable protein or TVP was something Melanie hated using, going so far as to never use it in the mixes she put up for sale, but they could make the recipe so people could use it if they wanted.

"I have some fresh from the freeze-dryer carrots and some split peas. I figured we'd use some of our bouillon, the low-sodium kind."

"Only one way to find out how that will turn out," Abigail said, already bustling around the kitchen, gathering pots and tools with the ease of someone who had spent countless hours in this space, transforming raw ingredients into magic.

Melanie joined in, her movements synchronized with Abigail's. They were two halves of a well-oiled machine. Every recipe was an adventure. Melanie couldn't imagine spending this much time with anyone other than Abigail.

As the soup began to simmer, filling the room with its hearty aroma, Melanie found herself hopeful. She glanced at Abigail, whose passion for culinary innovation knew no bounds, and felt a surge of gratitude for the friend who stood by her side, through thick and thin, purees and broths.

"All right, chef, let's make some magic," Melanie said, a spark of excitement igniting within her as they embarked on their latest gastronomic venture together.

Within a few hours, they had four burners going on their commercial stove, each of them with a different recipe for split pea soup. One had the full salt version of bouillon, another had the low salt, another was completely salt-free and the fourth had double the ham. Melanie hovered over the stove, absently stirring the split pea soup while lost in thought. The spoon moved in lazy circles, barely disturbing the surface. She was a portrait of distraction, her usually keen eyes staring through the rising steam as if it held life's answers.

"Earth to Melanie," Abigail said, snapping her fingers to recapture her friend's attention. "You've been quiet since I walked in. Even for a Tuesday, this is not your usual spark. What's up?"

Melanie set the wooden spoon down, leaning back against the counter with a soft sigh. Her gaze finally settled on Abigail, the corners of her mouth turned down in a rare display of vulnerability.

"Abby, I'm just... overwhelmed." The words came out in a rush, like a dam breaking. "Between managing the plant, developing new recipes, and dealing with suppliers, there's no time left for me. For...finding someone." Melanie shook her head. "I have so little downtime, but when I do have some, I wish there was someone beside me, you know? I can delegate so much of what I do to others, as long as I'm willing to watch over everything, but I can't delegate finding someone to..."

"Someone special, you mean?" Abigail leaned close, her voice dipped in empathy.

"Exactly. It feels like, with Melanie's Meals, I've bitten off more than I can chew," she confessed. "I want to fall in love, have that connection, but my schedule is a puzzle with missing pieces. Trying to coordinate that with someone else's? Might as well solve a jigsaw blindfolded."

"Hey, you're the queen of puzzles," Abigail countered, touching her arm reassuringly. "If anyone can figure it out, it's you."

"I wish it were that simple," Melanie said. "I want more than just a fleeting romance, Abby. I want someone who isn't afraid to get their hands dirty on the farm, who understands the work we do here."

"Then we'll find a way to make space for love in your schedule, Mel. You've built an empire from the ground up; how hard can dating be?"

"Harder than freeze-drying peas, apparently," Melanie quipped. Together, they returned their focus to the simmering pots before them.

Melanie stirred the pot before her, the gentle bubbling of the soup syncing with her thoughts. Abigail leaned against the kitchen counter, eyes narrowing as she watched her friend.

"Mel, you remember my cousin Alexis, right?" Abigail said, breaking the quiet rhythm of the simmering soup. "She got married recently."

Melanie turned, spoon still in hand. "Alexis? Didn't she end up with a father she knew nothing about and inherited a huge ranch from him?"

"That's the one," Abigail nodded, a mysterious twinkle in her eye. "Well, she did something radical. She met her husband at the altar."

Melanie's eyebrows shot up. "At the altar? Like...no dating, straight to marriage?"

"Exactly!" Abigail exclaimed. "There's this woman with a doctorate in psychology, Dr. Lachele Simpson. She does intense psychological testing and matches people who are compatible. They meet for the first time on their wedding day. It's crazy, but..." She shrugged. "Alexis is happy."

A laugh escaped Melanie's lips, part disbelief, part enchantment. "You're telling me they skipped the whole dating circus? Just...leap of faith, meet at the altar, and say 'I do'?"

"Yep. And they're disgustingly happy."

The wheels turned in Melanie's head, that spark of hope flickering to life. It was unorthodox, yes, but so was starting a business from freeze-dried vegetables. She grabbed her phone from the kitchen island, her fingers dancing over the screen with newfound urgency. "What was her name again?"

"Dr. Lachele Simpson."

"Right." Melanie hit the call button, and the line trilled once, twice, before a warm, slightly distracted voice answered.

"Dr. Lachele speaking."

"Hi, Dr. Lachele, it's Melanie Carter. A cousin of Alexis gave me your number. I heard about your...unique service."

"Ah, yes. I'd be delighted to help you find your match. How does this weekend sound for a consultation?"

"This weekend?" Melanie repeated, her heart skipping a beat. Could it be that simple? She thought about her obligations for the weekend, and decided to delegate the bulk of it. It wasn't something she often did, but she could do it once without feeling too horribly guilty.

"Yes! Where are you? No time like the present, right?"

"Right," Melanie said, a smile spreading across her face. "Let's do it."

"Fantastic. My cell grabbed your phone number, and I'll send you the details. Looking forward to meeting you, Melanie."

"Me too, Dr. Lachele. Thank you."

As she ended the call, Melanie looked at Abigail, her excitement barely contained. "She's coming this weekend."

"See?" Abigail grinned. "Sometimes the universe listens."

"Or sometimes, you just need to make the call," Melanie replied, feeling as if she'd just added the missing ingredient to a recipe she'd been perfecting for years.

"Needs more salt," Melanie decreed after a spoonful of their third pot.

"Or maybe a pinch of thyme?" Abigail suggested, her own culinary genius shining through in her deft adjustments to the recipe.

"Thyme! Of course," Melanie agreed, her taste buds already imagining the subtle difference the herb would make. They were in sync, two friends creating harmony in a bowl, one ingredient at a time.

Batches four through six blurred together, a dance of trial and error that left their kitchen smelling like an herb garden. The seventh batch was different, though. As they sipped cautiously from their spoons, their eyes met and held. No words were necessary; this was it.

"Split pea with carrots and barley," Melanie declared triumphantly. "It's hearty, it's flavorful—it's perfect!"

"Definitely our best batch yet," Abigail confirmed, her grin echoing Melanie's satisfaction.

Their hands met in a triumphant high five, the smack resonating in the warm kitchen. Laughter bubbled forth, not just for the successful recipe, but for the shared joy of accomplishment and the promise of what lay ahead.

"Here's to love, happiness, and the perfect split pea soup," Melanie said, raising her spoon like a toast.

"And to creating your destiny," Abigail added, clinking her spoon against Melanie's.

As the laughter faded, Melanie's green eyes sparkled with confidence and hope, mirroring the vibrant life she had cultivated. She had found success in her business, and now, she was ready to embrace whatever crazy, wonderful thing love had in store for her.

LUCAS BARNETT SAT IN the stillness of his spacious corner office, the only sound the muted hum of New York City life that filtered through the glass. From the 42nd floor, he watched as tiny figures scuttled along the sidewalks, ants marching in and out of towering monuments of steel and glass. He should have felt like a king, but instead, there was a hollow ache—a yearning for something indefinable.

He leaned back in his leather chair, a silent observer of the world below, where life surged forward with relentless energy. Yet in his chest, there was only an oppressive weight, a constant reminder that no amount of success could fill the void left by his wife's absence. It had been two years since she'd slipped away.

"Is this really it?" Lucas whispered to himself, his voice barely disturbing the silence of the room.

"Where do I go from here?" The question tumbled from his lips. For the first time in a long while, Lucas allowed himself to acknowledge the depth of his loss.

With a deep breath, he stood up and approached the window, pressing a hand against the cool surface. The city, with its ceaseless pulse, suddenly felt like a stranger. And in that moment, Lucas understood that maybe what he needed most wasn't to reclaim what he had lost, but to discover who he could become.

Lucas turned from the window. His dark brown hair gave him an air of distinction, and the broad set of his shoulders suggested a man who was accustomed to bearing heavy burdens with grace.

He paused by his mahogany desk, his reflection staring back at him from the framed family photo perched on its edge.

"Enough," he whispered to himself. New York City could no longer contain him. Lucas needed space to breathe, room to grow beyond the persona of the widower.

The decision formed with surprising clarity, like a skyscraper emerging from a foggy skyline. He would leave this all behind: the high-rise office, the penthouse apartment, the streets he walked with her. Lucas needed a fresh canvas, a place where her shadow didn't darken every doorway, where he could sketch out a new chapter—one filled with possibilities rather than haunted by regrets.

"Psychologists in New York City," he murmured as he typed, the words a whispered incantation inviting change. The list unfurled on his phone like a scroll, names and faces promising guidance and understanding. Then, one particular photo caught his eye and held it—an image so out of place in the sea of professional headshots that it might as well have been a beacon.

Dr. Lachele Simpson gazed back at him from the screen, her purple hair a vibrant statement against the backdrop of diplomas and credentials adorning her office wall. There was something about her smile that reached out. Her attire was an impeccable balance between professionalism and personality—sharp lines softened by the whimsical hue atop her head.

"Maybe you're the one," Lucas said. It was not just her striking appearance that drew him in. Her bio mentioned a unique approach to healing, one that veered from the traditional path much like he intended to do. She was a middle-aged maverick in a field of conformity, and Lucas felt a kinship with the idea of defying expectations.

He filled out the contact form, his fingers steady but his heart pounding. This was the first concrete step toward his new life. He hit 'send' and leaned back in his chair, allowing himself a moment to envision meeting this Dr. Lachele Simpson, wondering if her presence was as commanding as her online persona suggested.

"Here goes nothing," Lucas exhaled.

Lucas Barnett stood on the sidewalk, watching as an Uber guided Dr. Lachele Simpson to the curb. He recognized her instantly from the vibrant purple streaks in her hair, even as it danced wildly in the breeze.

Dr. Simpson emerged from the car, her professional attire stark against her unconventional hair. He walked to her. "Are you Dr. Simpson?"

Lachele smiled. "Yes, but everyone just calls me Dr. Lachele. You're Mr. Barnett?"

He nodded. "Yes, I am." Taking a deep breath, he pushed open the door to her office, stepping from the concrete jungle into a sanctuary of calm designed for unraveling the knots in troubled minds.

"Please come in." Her voice was warm, inviting, and punctuated by the click of her heels on hardwood as she approached.

"Lucas, please," he corrected, shaking her hand. His grip was firm, but he felt the tremor of anticipation coursing through him.

"Lucas then," she smiled, leading him to a cozy seating area. "What brings you here today?"

He took a seat, sinking into the plush fabric, and met her gaze, which held a measure of curiosity that seemed to coax the words from him.

"I'm looking for a fresh start," he began. "I've built a life here in the city, but since my wife passed, I've felt lost, like I'm just going through the motions."

Dr. Simpson nodded, her expression one of understanding rather than pity. "A new beginning can be a powerful thing," she said thoughtfully.

"Exactly," Lucas affirmed, finding strength in her agreement. "I want to move forward, to find purpose again, but I don't even know where to begin."

"Sometimes, beginning is as simple as deciding to do so."

"Which is why I'm here," Lucas added quickly. "I heard about your unique approach, and I think it's exactly what I need."

"Then let's explore the possibilities together," Dr. Simpson offered with an encouraging nod, her purple hair catching the light as she moved.

Lucas could feel the layers of doubt and grief peeling back, revealing a spark of hope. He knew he was ready to embrace the unknown, to chase after happiness wherever it might lead—As long as it was outside of this city full of memories.

"Lucas," Dr. Simpson began, "I think you've taken enough time to grieve. You're right. It's time to start a new life, and I have an idea for you."

He found himself leaning in, drawn by the authenticity in her tone.

"I use my degree in a way most don't. I have a business where I am a matchmaker."

"Dr. Simpson..." he hesitated. The idea was preposterous, wasn't it?

"Call me Lachele," she interjected gently. "And please, go on."

"It's just that...I'm afraid of taking the wrong step, of making a mistake in this search for a new beginning."

"What I offer is a matchmaking program," she revealed. "But not like anything you've encountered before. You see, I believe that love can be both a science and an art. I put candidates through eight hours of psychological testing to find their best match—the one person who complements them in every essential way."

She paused, allowing the enormity of her proposal to settle between them.

"Here's the catch," she added, a playful twinkle dancing in her eye, "you don't meet your partner until the moment you stand together at the altar."

Lucas blinked. The idea was radical, daunting even. Yet the spark of intrigue couldn't be denied, fanning the embers of hope that had lain dormant in his chest for far too long.

"The altar?" he echoed.

"Yes," Lachele confirmed. "It's about trust, Lucas. Trusting the process, trusting yourself, and yes, trusting a complete stranger to become an integral part of your life."

The room seemed to pulse with possibility, the city's endless rhythm a distant echo compared to the beat of potential drumming in his own heart. Could he possibly do it?

Lucas leaned forward, elbows on his knees, the words 'altar' and 'trust' circling in his head like birds of prey. They swooped down, sharp and demanding attention, forcing him to confront the skepticism rooted deep within. "It sounds...unconventional."

"Life is anything but conventional, Lucas," Dr. Lachele Simpson replied. "Sometimes, it's the unorthodox paths that lead us to the most fulfilling destinations."

He raked a hand through his hair, the gesture betraying his inner turmoil. The idea of marrying a stranger was ludicrous—a leap of faith so vast it bordered on absurdity. Yet, wasn't it that very absurdity that tugged at him, whispering promises of change?

"Tell me," he asked, voice steadier than he felt, "how often does it work out? This...matchmaking of yours?"

"In ten years, there's yet to be a divorce," she answered. "I've seen it rekindle hope, bring new life. Isn't that what you're looking for?"

Lucas nodded. "All right," he said finally. "Let's do it."

"Truly?" Dr. Lachele's eyebrows arched in pleasant surprise. She didn't see him as a man who took risks.

"Yes," Lucas said. Maybe he was losing his mind, but it was time he did something different...something dangerous even. "Thank you," he said earnestly, meeting Dr. Lachele's vibrant eyes. "For offering a path I hadn't considered."

"Thank yourself," she returned the handshake firmly, "for having the courage to walk it."

As Lucas walked the distance to his high-rise apartment, he felt that he was finally doing something right. He could relocate anywhere. And he was determined to be happy.

He walked with purpose, his strides long and sure, weaving through the crowds with an ease born from years of navigating this urban maze. Yet, now, each footfall seemed to echo with the promise of a future somewhere far removed from the concrete canyons of Manhattan.

Lucas paused at a crosswalk, waiting for the light to change. He looked up at the skyscrapers reaching for the heavens, reflecting on how they once symbolized his dreams and aspirations. Now, they were just signposts pointing him toward a new life.

A new life somewhere—anywhere—else.

Chapter Two

Melanie Carter stood at the back of a small, charming church tucked away in the small town of Deep Valley, Missouri. The stained-glass windows cast a kaleidoscope of colors across her white wedding dress, making the silk fabric shimmer like a carefully constructed illusion. She clasped her hands together, fingers entwined so tightly that her knuckles turned white.

"Abigail," Melanie whispered, turning to her best friend who was clad in a blush-toned bridesmaid dress. "I think I've lost my mind."

"Hey," Abigail said gently, stepping closer. She laid a reassuring hand on Melanie's slender shoulder, grounding her. "You haven't lost anything, least of all your mind. You're just nervous, that's all. It's normal."

Melanie let out a breath, her eyes scanning the empty pews, the altar adorned with flowers, and the quiet anticipation that filled the air. "I might have to run for it. Sprint down the aisle, out the door, and never look back." She held up a foot adorned with bright white sneakers. "I'm dressed for it!"

"Melanie Carter," Abigail chided with a soft chuckle, "the day you run from a challenge will be the day I dye my hair green and take up yodeling." Her tone was light, but her gaze held Melanie's with unwavering sincerity. "You're the bravest person I know. You took over your grandmother's farm, built it into a thriving business from scratch. You're not going to bolt because of cold feet."

Melanie's lips curved upward in a tentative smile, encouraged by Abigail's belief in her. The fluttering in her stomach settled, if only marginally. "It's just... this is the biggest jigsaw puzzle of my life, and I don't even have the picture on the box to help me put it together."

"Think of it this way," Abigail replied, tucking a stray curl behind Melanie's ear. "You're about to meet your missing piece." Her eyes gleamed with excitement. "And I bet he's just as perfect for you as thyme is for your roasted garlic mushrooms."

Her attempt at humor worked, drawing a genuine laugh from Melanie. For a moment, they were not in a church poised on the edge of a life-altering event. Instead, they were back in the farmhouse kitchen, dusted with flour, surrounded by the fragrance of their first culinary creation.

"Okay," Melanie breathed out, steadying herself with a nod. "Let's do this. No running, no hiding. Just...forward."

"That's my girl," Abigail beamed, squeezing Melanie's hands before letting go. "Now, let's get you married."

With a newfound resolve, Melanie smoothed down her dress, lifted her chin, and stepped toward her future—one careful, hopeful pace at a time.

Melanie's shoes squeaked against the marble aisle, a metronome to her racing heart as she approached the altar. The white pews blurred into a sea of expectant faces, but her gaze was on the man who stood waiting.

Lucas Barnett's salt-and-pepper hair distinguished him from the younger crowd yet did nothing to diminish his commanding presence. His broad shoulders, cloaked in a charcoal suit, seemed to bear the weight of expectation effortlessly. As Melanie drew closer, she could see the faint lines around his eyes—not wrinkles, but markers of laughter and loss.

Their eyes met, and for a moment, the world fell away. There was no church, no guests, just two people on either side of an unseen bridge. Lucas extended his hand, palm open and inviting, and Melanie placed hers within it, feeling a surprising warmth that steadied her trembling fingers.

"Lucas," he introduced himself, his voice deep.

"Melanie." Her reply was a whisper, almost lost in the cavernous space, but he heard it, a small smile tugging at the corner of his mouth.

"Nice to finally meet you," Lucas said, the corners of his eyes crinkling with sincerity.

"Likewise," Melanie answered, her initial nervousness giving way to a burgeoning curiosity about the man before her. She noticed how his thumb gently brushed against her hand, a touch so brief yet unexpectedly comforting.

The officiant cleared his throat, a subtle cue that snapped them back to reality. Melanie took her position beside Lucas, aware of the many eyes upon them.

As the ceremony began, Melanie allowed herself a quick study of Lucas. He seemed as at ease in his suit as she felt in her yoga pants and t-shirts daily.

"Lucas," the officiant prompted, "do you take Melanie to be your lawfully wedded wife?"

"I do," he said, and his grip on her hand tightened ever so slightly.

"Melanie, do you take Lucas to be your lawfully wedded husband?"

"I do," she echoed, and the words felt like the first piece of the puzzle falling into place.

In the space between "I do" and the sealing kiss, Melanie saw in Lucas's eyes a reflection of her determination—a shared recognition that they were stepping into uncharted territory.

The final blessing was pronounced, and the congregation erupted into applause as Lucas and Melanie turned to face them—husband and wife in the eyes of the world, strangers in each other's gaze. The walk down the aisle was a blur of smiling faces and a cascade of flower petals, their hands still clasped together like an anchor amidst the sea of celebration.

In the quiet back room of the church, the newlyweds found a moment of respite from the whirlwind ceremony. Surrounded by the soft hum of muffled conversations seeping through the walls, they sat on a plain bench.

Lucas took a deep breath, his mind grappling with the reality of being married to this woman. There was a tangible sense of expectation hanging in the air, and as he glanced at Melanie, she met his gaze with a solemn nod, as if acknowledging the gravity of their shared leap of faith.

"Lucas," Melanie began her voice steady but laced with underlying excitement, "I run a business. It started small, just me with a freeze-dryer, a dehydrator and my grandmother's recipes. But now it's...it's more than I ever dreamed."

She hesitated for a moment, collecting her thoughts. "We freeze-dry farm produce, create recipes—it's grown into a whole plant and warehouse operation. And I..." She paused, looking into his eyes, searching for a hint of understanding or approval. "I'd like for you to consider being a part of it, handling the farming aspect."

He looked at her for a moment and a laugh bubbled up. "I've been the CFO of a Fortune 500 Company for the past ten years, and now I'm going to farm. I love the idea!"

Melanie's eyes widened. "Are you sure?"

"Melanie," he said, "I came here ready to start over, to cultivate something meaningful. Your company, your vision—I want to learn more. I want to see where this path leads us."

Relief washed over Melanie's features, her shoulders relaxing as she leaned slightly toward him. The tension that had knotted her insides began to unravel, replaced by the budding warmth of potential partnership and mutual respect.

"Thank you," she whispered, her gratitude genuine, "for being willing to take this risk with me."

The sounds of celebration beckoned from beyond the door, a melody of laughter and clinking glasses underscored by the soft hum of conversation. Melanie's fingers fluttered to her lips, the remnants of nerves dissipating like mist in sunlight, as Lucas stood facing her.

"Shall we?" he asked, a hand extended toward her. But there was a hesitation in his eyes.

She placed her hand in his, feeling the reassuring warmth of his palm. "Let's not keep them waiting," Melanie replied with a burgeoning smile. Yet, neither moved toward the festivities. Instead, they stood still, caught in an orbit of their own making.

"Melanie," Lucas began. "Before we go out there, I want you to know—"

He didn't finish his sentence; words became unnecessary as he leaned in, his gaze locked onto hers. Melanie found herself drawn in, the world narrowing down to the space where their breaths mingled. His lips met hers in a gentle collision, a kiss that was tentative at first as if testing the waters of this new reality they found themselves in.

But then it deepened, grew confident—a silent affirmation of the leap they had taken together. The kiss spoke of beginnings, of hope, and the thrill of shared dreams. It was a seal over the vows they'd just exchanged, a private moment in a day that belonged to everyone but them.

As they parted, their foreheads rested against each other for a heartbeat, eyes opening to reveal matching expressions of wonder. There was no fanfare, no grand gesture—just two souls finding comfort in the quiet assurance of what might be.

"Come on, Mr. and Mrs. for the first time in public," Melanie said with a playful glint in her eye, the corners of her mouth curving upwards.

Lucas chuckled, the sound rich and warm. He squeezed her hand, and together they turned toward the door, ready to join the world that awaited them.

Abigail had transformed the church hall into a tableau of elegance and joy. Strings of fairy lights wove through the rafters, casting a golden glow over the assembled guests. Tables adorned with centerpieces of delicate flowers and candles created an ambiance of rustic charm that was both welcoming and intimate.

"Wow, Abigail outdid herself," Melanie murmured, taking in the sight.

"Abigail has quite the talent," Lucas agreed, his admiration evident. They were greeted by applause and cheers, a cacophony of well-wishes that enveloped them like a warm embrace. Abigail emerged from the crowd, her face alight with excitement.

"Congratulations, you two!" she exclaimed, pulling Melanie in for a hug. "Everything okay? You both disappeared for a bit."

"Everything's perfect," Melanie assured her, exchanging a knowing look with Lucas.

"Good! Now go, mingle, eat, dance! This is your party," Abigail instructed with a laugh, shooing them gently into the throng of family and friends.

As they made their rounds, accepting congratulations and sharing laughs, Melanie couldn't help but feel that this—this was the beginning of something truly extraordinary. With Lucas by her side, anything seemed possible.

The tires of Melanie's old pickup truck crunched over the gravel as they approached the farmhouse, its pale yellow paint glowing under the Missouri moonlight. The day's excitement had settled into a comfortable silence between them, with only the occasional rustle of fabric and soft sigh punctuating the tranquility.

"Here we are," Melanie said as she pulled the keys from the ignition, her voice tinged with pride. "Home."

Lucas stepped out of the truck, his gaze sweeping across the wide-open spaces that stretched toward the horizon. There was something undeniably peaceful about this place, vastly different from the never-ending buzz of New York City. He followed Melanie up the creaky wooden steps to the porch, where the swing swayed gently in the night breeze.

Melanie led him through the front door, flicking on lights as they went. The interior was a cozy mix of modern and rustic, the air filled with the faint scent of vanilla. She showed him the living room, with its plush sofa and bookshelves brimming with literature, then the kitchen where copper pots hung above the island like silent sentinels.

"And this," she said, stopping before a door at the end of the hallway, "is your room." She opened it to reveal a modest space with a large window overlooking the fields. A quilt, patterned with squares of vibrant color, lay neatly folded at the foot of the bed.

"It's perfect," Lucas replied genuinely, setting his overnight bag down. "Thank you, Melanie."

They stood there for a moment, the weight of the day's events settling around them like dust. It was Melanie who broke the silence. "I know today was unconventional, even a bit crazy," she started, her eyes searching his. "But I hope you'll find happiness here, with me, with the farm... and maybe one day, with us."

Lucas's heart responded with a quiet leap. He crossed the small space between them and took her hands in his. "I came here looking to start over, to find purpose again," he said. "And standing here with you, I believe I've made the right choice."

"Good," she smiled, her relief palpable. "Because I want you to be part of this—my life, my business, everything. But...we'll take it one step at a time."

"One step at a time," Lucas echoed, nodding. They shared a look, an unspoken agreement that they would move forward together, but at their own pace. There was no rush; after all, they had a lifetime ahead of them to figure out the rhythm of their dance.

"Come on," Melanie said after a beat. "Let me show you the rest of the house. And then, maybe, if you're not too tired, I can beat you at a jigsaw puzzle."

"Challenge accepted," Lucas replied with a laugh, following her back down the hall.

As he followed her through the charming farmhouse, he said a silent prayer that they would find what they were looking for together, and that life would be kind to them.

Chapter Three

Melanie moved with a purpose, her slender frame navigating the space between stove and counter like a dancer in her element. The sizzle of bacon filled the air with a comforting aroma, mingling with the sweet scent of pancakes that browned on the griddle.

"Hope you're hungry," Melanie called out, turning to where Lucas leaned casually against the doorframe. His hair was tousled from sleep, exuding an easy charm that belied his recent upheaval.

"Starving," he admitted with a smile that reached his eyes, watching as Melanie expertly flipped a pancake. "It smells incredible. I think the country air is making me hungrier!"

"Breakfast is the most important meal of the day," she said. She plated a heap of scrambled eggs alongside crispy bacon strips and golden pancakes, then set the generous meal before him.

As they ate, Melanie's gaze occasionally swept the room, double-checking everything was in place—a habit born from years of ensuring her business ran smoothly.

"Ready for the grand tour?" Melanie asked once their plates were clean, her voice tinged with excitement that seemed to fill the kitchen with sunlight.

"Lead the way," Lucas replied, eager to discover more about this new world he was stepping into. He hadn't expected her to have a job for him, and he was excited to learn all there was to know about farming. It would certainly be the change he was looking for.

Outside rows of crops swayed gently in the breeze. As they walked, Melanie's red hair caught the sun, a fiery banner against the green expanse. She stopped by the chicken coop, motioning for Lucas to follow.

"Here's where we gather eggs every morning," she explained, demonstrating how to reach under the hens without causing a ruckus. Her movements were deft and sure, and Lucas mimicked them, feeling a sense of accomplishment when he cradled the warm eggs in his hands.

"Looks like you've got the hang of it," Melanie remarked, a hint of approval in her tone.

They moved on, Melanie pointing out the various crops—tomatoes reaching for the sky, zucchini hiding beneath broad leaves, and berries adding pops of color. She spoke of each plant as if it were an old friend, sharing tidbits of knowledge that Lucas absorbed eagerly.

"Never thought I'd find myself farming," Lucas confessed, brushing a hand through his hair, leaving a streak of dirt that Melanie found endearing. "Definitely a change from the spreadsheets I'm used to."

"Life has a funny way of taking us places we never expected," she mused, her voice softening as she shared a piece of her own journey. "I always thought I'd end up being a teacher, but just before I was supposed to start college, my grandmother died, leaving me this farm. My friend Abigail and I put our heads together and came up with the idea to freeze-dry our ingredients. And Deep Valley Harvest was born. Melanie's Meals came a few years late because we loved creating recipes together so much. What started as a cottage industry where I sold things at farmer's markets has become a full-fledged business complete with a warehouse and a plant. It's taken me ten years to get here, but I'm pleased with where my business is going."

Lucas listened, the seeds of understanding and respect taking root between them, growing with each word exchanged. The farm was not just land and labor; it was Melanie's legacy, her passion—and he was going to make it his new beginning.

Melanie led Lucas past a row of fragrant herbs, her boots sinking into the rich soil that she had come to know like the back of her hand. The sun was climbing higher, draping the farm in a warm, golden light that made the dew on the leaves shimmer.

"Most of these fields are planted with crops we sell directly through Deep Valley Harvest," Melanie said, her voice laced with pride as her gaze swept over the expanse. "We work with local farmers too. They grow specific varieties that thrive here in Missouri, and then sell their yield to us."

Lucas squinted against the brightness of the morning sun, following Melanie's pointed finger to a distant plot of land where rows upon rows of leafy greens waved gently in the breeze. "So, it's like a community effort?"

"Exactly," Melanie affirmed, a smile curving her lips. "It's all about supporting each other and providing for the community. We make sure nothing goes to waste, and everyone gets their fair share."

They walked in companionable silence until they reached a small clearing shaded by an old oak tree. Here, Melanie paused, turning to face Lucas with an animated sparkle in her eyes. "And then there's Melanie's Meals. That's my baby. Abigail and I spend hours in the kitchen, experimenting with flavors, creating recipes that anyone can make at home."

"Abigail must be quite the cook if she's your right-hand woman in this," Lucas said, intrigued.

"She's a culinary wizard," Melanie chuckled. "Between the two of us, we've turned family favorites into easy-to-prepare meal kits that we sell online. It's not just food—it's about bringing people together, one meal at a time."

Lucas nodded, impressed. "I guess it takes more than just knowing how to farm to run a business like yours."

"Sure does," Melanie replied. "But it's worth it when you see the impact you're making—not only on the dinner tables but in the lives of the farmers and the community."

Their conversation was a gentle ebb and flow, and as they continued to walk the property, Lucas couldn't help but feel a swelling sense of hope. With Melanie at his side, guiding him through the intricacies of her world, the daunting prospect of taking on farming seemed less intimidating, perhaps even possible.

As they moved toward the next task, Melanie's laughter harmonized with the rustle of leaves, painting the air with the melody of a life filled with purpose and the promise of new beginnings.

Melanie led Lucas past the rows of vibrant crops, her basket swinging lightly in her grasp. She stopped before a patch of lush, green stalks that stood tall and proud against the horizon.

"Every part of this farm has a story," she said, bending down to snap off several stalks of celery with practiced ease. "These might end up in one of our meal kits or sold fresh at the local market."

Lucas watched as she placed the celery carefully into the basket. "You really do it all here, don't you?"

"Almost," Melanie replied with a knowing smile. "But for the bigger tasks, I have a team at the plant. Jacob Sallinger manages the day-to-day operations there. He's been a cornerstone of the operation since we expanded from the kitchen table to an actual production facility."

"Sounds like you've got good people on your side," Lucas observed, the corners of his mouth lifting slightly.

"Couldn't do it without them," she admitted, leading the way back toward the farmhouse. The sun was climbing higher now, its warmth seeping into their skin as they walked.

Once inside the coolness of her home, Melanie set the basket on the counter and pulled out a couple of the freshest celery stalks. "Now, let me show you one of my favorite things to do with these."

Lucas leaned against the doorframe, his arms folded across his chest as he watched her with interest. She retrieved a tray and arranged the celery with a precision that spoke of countless hours spent perfecting the technique. With a flourish, she slid the tray into a sleek machine nestled between other high-end kitchen appliances.

"Freeze drying," she explained, her fingers dancing over the controls. "It's a fantastic way to preserve produce. Keeps the flavor and nutrients locked in until you're ready to use it." She turned back to him. "This is the home freeze-dryer I first started with, but we have lots of commercial freeze dryers at the plant. This is our busy time of year as different things get ripe. There's enough work for the whole year, but there's lots of overtime now."

He raised an eyebrow, intrigued by the process. "How is that different from just tossing it in the freezer?"

"Completely," she assured him, her eyes sparkling with enthusiasm. "It's about reducing the water content without compromising the structure. You get the same taste and texture as fresh when you rehydrate it."

"Never knew celery could be so interesting," Lucas quipped, the corner of his mouth quirking up.

"Wait until you try it in one of our mixes," Melanie laughed, her voice filled with the confidence of someone who knew the value of her work. "You'll be surprised how something so simple can transform a dish."

The machine hummed to life, and Melanie stepped back, brushing a loose strand of red hair behind her ear. In that moment, surrounded by the fruits of her labor, she seemed to Lucas the very embodiment of modern ambition mixed with traditional values.

"All right, enough about freeze drying," she said, her tone shifting back to business. "Let's talk dinner plans. How do you feel about chicken fettuccini alfredo tonight?"

"From one of your special mixes?" Lucas asked, already anticipating the flavors.

"Exactly," Melanie confirmed, her laughter ringing clear and hopeful in the kitchen. "You won't believe how good it is until you've tried it."

As the machine continued its quiet whir, Melanie shared more about her vision for the farm and her company. Each word painted a picture of a future ripe with possibilities, and Lucas found himself drawn into the dream she wove.

"See, freeze drying and dehydrating are similar," she began, her voice tinged with the excitement of sharing knowledge. "But they're not twins. Dehydrating basically removes moisture by circulating warm air. It's sort of like drying clothes on a line under the sun." She tapped the machine. "Freeze drying, on the other hand, is like magic. It freezes the produce first and then reduces the surrounding pressure to allow the frozen water in the material to sublimate directly from the solid phase to the gas phase."

"Magic, huh?" Lucas chuckled, his arms crossed as he leaned against the doorframe, admiring the way Melanie's green eyes sparkled when she spoke about her passion.

"Absolutely," she replied, closing the lid with a satisfying click. "It keeps the cell structure intact, preserving the nutritional content and taste. Think of it like this: dehydration gives you a chewy snack, while freeze drying provides that perfect crunch and original flavor." Her hands moved with a flourish, as if she were casting the spell she described. "We use both in our products, but we specialize in freeze-drying."

"Sounds impressive," Lucas nodded, but a crease formed between his brows as a different kind of worry settled over him. "But I'm no magician, Melanie. Are you sure you want me taking over the farming? I can barely tell a weed from a vegetable."

Melanie turned to face him, her expression earnest. There was a brief silence as she considered his doubt, her gaze steady. "Lucas, I don't expect you to be an expert overnight. It's not just about knowing plants. It's about understanding them and caring for them. That's something I believe you're more than capable of."

He looked down at his boots, feeling the weight of responsibility and the fear of failing at something so foreign to him. Yet, there was something in Melanie's tone, a thread of confidence that wove itself around his uncertainties and tugged gently.

"Besides," Melanie continued, a playful glint in her eye, "anyone who has successfully navigated New York City can surely learn the ways of Missouri soil."

Her words, light yet laden with faith, chipped away at the wall of his apprehension. Lucas straightened, the broad set of his shoulders squaring as he met her gaze.

"All right," he said after a moment, his voice carrying a newfound determination. "I'll give it my all. For the farm, for the future...and for us."

Melanie's smile spread slowly. "That's all I ask," she replied, her heart swelling with the hope that together, they could cultivate not just a thriving business, but also a love as enduring as the land itself.

Much later, Lucas followed Melanie into the kitchen, trailing her like a student shadowing a mentor. In the warm glow of the farmhouse lights, Melanie moved with purpose, reaching for a package from the pantry.

"Here," she said, holding out a neatly labeled pouch. "Let's get dinner started. It's one of our best-selling mixes—chicken fettuccine alfredo."

He took the pouch, turning it over in his hands. "You make this too?"

"Yep, Abigail and I worked on perfecting the recipe. It's all about balancing flavors and making sure everything rehydrates correctly." She retrieved a pot from the cupboard, filling it with water before setting it on the stove.

"Seems like there's a lot to learn," Lucas admitted, watching her movements.

Melanie glanced back at him. "There is, but you don't have to know it all right now. What you need is the willingness to dig in, research, and ask tons of questions. You're starting with a clean slate, Lucas. Be curious, be eager. That's how we grow, in farming and in life."

"Curiosity I can do," he said, a corner of his mouth lifting in a small, appreciative smile.

"Good." Melanie's eyes twinkled. "Because that's exactly what brought me here—to this place where I can pour my heart into something that grows."

As the water began to boil, she poured in the contents of the mix. The aroma of herbs and garlic filled the room, wrapping around them like a warm blanket. Lucas watched, fascinated, as the once-dry ingredients came to life, swelling and melding into a creamy, inviting dish.

"From this to that," he murmured, gesturing to the transformation in the pot.

"Exactly. A little bit of magic," she quipped, giving the pasta a final stir before plating their meals.

They sat down at the rustic kitchen table, and Lucas forked a generous mouthful of the chicken fettuccine alfredo. As the flavors exploded on his tongue, his eyebrows shot up in surprise. "This is incredible, Melanie. Honestly, I wouldn't have guessed it came from a mix."

"Thank you." Pride laced her voice. "We put a lot of love into each recipe. It's not just about convenience; it's about creating something special that brings people together, even on their busiest days."

"Mission accomplished," he said, taking another bite. "I'm starting to think that maybe I can contribute something worthwhile to this place after all."

"You already are," she assured him, her gaze meeting his across the flickering candlelight. "Just by being willing to step into this new world with an open mind."

"What made you decide to contact Dr. Lachele?" he asked.

She laughed softly. "Isn't it obvious? I have no time for anything but my work. No time for dates. But by being married as soon as we met, I can involve you in the business, and we can learn about each other as you learn about what I do." She blew on the food overflowing her fork. "What about you?"

He took a deep breath. "I lost my wife two years ago. Everywhere I went in New York, I was reminded of her. I needed to get away or put up shrines to her. I still miss her every day, but I think it's time for me to move on. Finally."

Melanie nodded. "I can understand that. And rural Missouri is as different from NYC as you can get, I would imagine."

He nodded. "So far it sure is."

After the plates were cleared, Melanie guided Lucas to the living room, where an oversized couch and a large flat-screen TV awaited them. She selected a light-hearted romantic comedy from the streaming service queue—a tale of love found, lost, and rekindled in the heart of London, reflecting both the humor and hopefulness that colored their own circumstances.

"Hope you like 'Meet Me in Hyde Park,'" she said, pressing play.

"Never seen it," Lucas admitted, "but I'm game." He settled back against the cushions, his broad frame taking up one end of the couch as Melanie curled up at the other, tucking her feet beneath her.

The opening credits rolled amidst the backdrop of bustling city streets, accompanied by a jaunty tune that set the tone for the evening. As the protagonists' unlikely romance unfolded on screen, occasional laughter mingled with the film's dialogue. Glances were exchanged—shy, amused, and increasingly warm.

"Cities seem like they belong in a different world," Lucas mused during a lull in the movie.

"Sometimes, but I guess in some ways, it's not so different from here," Melanie replied. "People looking for connection, for a place where they belong."

"Finding where you belong..." He let the words trail off, his gaze drifting from the screen to catch Melanie's profile.

As the movie reached its inevitable happy ending, Lucas felt a contentment he hadn't known in a long while. The characters had found their place in each other's lives, and he wondered if perhaps he was starting to find his place here.

The screen faded to black, and they sat in companionable silence for a moment before Melanie stirred. "Well, that was fun," she said, stretching her arms above her head. "But we have an early start tomorrow."

"Right, the crack of dawn awaits," Lucas chuckled, pushing himself up from the couch. They moved together toward the hallway, their steps slow and reluctant to part.

"Your alarm's set?" she asked, her tone light but carrying the undercurrent of care that had become familiar to him in the short time he'd been here.

"Set and ready to jolt me awake at five," he assured her, his voice a mix of mock dread and genuine anticipation for the day ahead.

"Good." Melanie paused at the door to his guest room, her hand resting lightly on the doorknob. "And Lucas? If you need anything, just holler. My room is just across the hall."

"Thank you, Melanie. For everything." He offered her a smile, one that spoke volumes of the gratitude and respect he held for her.

"Goodnight, Lucas."

"Goodnight," he echoed, watching as she turned to go to her own room.

As Lucas entered his room, it occurred to him that he wasn't just learning about farming or freeze-dried celery. He was learning about life's second chances—and maybe, just maybe, about love reborn. With that thought, he closed his door and prepared himself for bed. And for tomorrow and all the tomorrows to come.

Chapter Four

Melanie slid her keys off the hook by the door and shot a glance at Lucas. "Ready to see where the magic happens?" Her voice, always direct, carried an undercurrent of pride.

"Absolutely," Lucas replied, his smile genuine. They stepped out into the cool morning air of mid-June as they made their way to her truck.

The drive was short but filled with purposeful conversation, Melanie outlining the day's agenda while Lucas listened intently, nodding as he mentally prepared himself for the overview of her bustling enterprise.

Pulling into the plant parking lot, Melanie parked the car, and they both stepped out. The rhythmic hum of productivity greeted them even before they entered the plant—a symphony of mechanical whirs and human activity.

As the metal doors swung open, Lucas took it all in: the vast expanse of the warehouse unfolded before him, a hive of ceaseless motion. Conveyor belts transported neatly sealed packages toward their final destinations, while forklifts wove between the aisles with balletic precision. Employees, their faces set in concentration, maneuvered around the machinery, monitoring the production process with practiced ease. "We work three shifts per day at this time of year," she said. "From mid-May through late October, we're in constant motion, with the harvesting, drying, and packaging of products. Many items are packaged to sell immediately, but many more are set aside in barrels to be used when we make our mixes, which mostly happens in the late fall to early spring. Abigail and I put together a recipe for split pea soup a month ago, and we'll have that coming off the belts in another month. I'll post the recipe and announce the sale of the packaged soup mixes at the same time."

"Wow, you weren't kidding about having this place humming," Lucas commented, raising his voice slightly over the din of industry.

Melanie beamed at him, her slender form cutting through the organized chaos like she owned every inch—which, of course, she did. "It took years to get to this point. Every detail matters, from the sourcing of our ingredients to the quality control on that packaging line over there." She gestured toward a group meticulously inspecting the freeze-dried products before they were packaged.

Lucas's gaze followed her pointing finger, noting the care with which each employee handled the goods. Their dedication was palpable, a reflection of the respect and loyalty Melanie had clearly cultivated within her team.

"Everything is interconnected," Melanie continued, leading him further into the heart of operations. "And every person here plays a crucial role in bringing our products from farm to table—or should I say, from farm to shelf."

He smiled, impressed not only by the scale of her ambitions realized in concrete and steel but also by the passion that laced her words. It was contagious, that blend of entrepreneurial spirit and personal investment. As they walked, Melanie's red hair caught the light streaming in through the skylights, an ember amidst the machinery.

"Let me show you the production floor up close," she said, her stride never faltering as Lucas kept pace. "You'll get to see exactly what goes into making our freeze-dried goods so special."

"Lead the way," Lucas said, already captivated by the intricate dance of productivity—and by the woman who orchestrated it all. To his knowledge, he'd never tried freeze-dried food before the previous evening, and he had been surprised at just how good it was.

Lucas followed Melanie into a brightly lit corner of the warehouse where a woman with an infectious smile and a chef's apron bustled among stainless steel tables laden with vibrant food products. Abigail Lindstrom, her nametag cheerfully declared, looked up from her meticulous work and broke into a wide grin upon seeing them.

"Ah, you must be Lucas!" she said, extending a flour-dusted hand which he took, noting the firmness of her grip that spoke of years kneading and mixing. "I'm Abby, Melanie's right hand in all things culinary."

"Didn't I see you at the reception?" Lucas asked, his own confidence meeting her enthusiasm. "Melanie's told me a bit about your magic with flavors."

"Magic is just the start of it," Abby chuckled, her eyes gleaming with pride. She waved them closer to a tray of colorful fruit pieces. "These are the latest batch ready for freeze-drying. We use low temperatures and a vacuum to extract moisture. It's all about locking in taste and texture without preservatives. Our berries stay tart, our mangoes sweet as summer—all while lasting longer than any fresh counterpart could dream."

Lucas picked up a slice of strawberry, its color still vividly red, and popped it into his mouth. The flavor exploded, intense and pure, a concentrated burst of summertime. "That's incredible," he admitted, genuinely impressed. "It's like the essence of the fruit is magnified."

"Exactly!" Abby's eyes sparkled. "Melanie has a real talent for spotting which products will benefit most from this process. And we're always experimenting."

She guided them to another table showcasing an array of Melanie's creations. Lucas's gaze lingered on a collection of packets labeled with bold letters: 'Freeze-Dried Ice Cream – Just Add Water!' Beside it were jars filled with powdered sauces, their colors ranging from a fiery orange to a deep burgundy.

"Here's where things get really fun," Abby said, unscrewing a jar of the powder. "This is a concentrated sauce base—just add water, and you've got a gourmet sauce in minutes. Perfect for camping trips or quick home-cooked meals."

"Melanie's idea?" Lucas asked, raising an eyebrow in admiration.

"Yup!" Abby confirmed. "Her vision's to make quality food accessible, no matter where you are. And wait till you try the ice cream." She handed him a small sachet. "Just imagine, astronauts eat something similar in space. You can have a scoop of rocky road on a mountain peak or in the comfort of your living room."

"Remarkable," Lucas murmured, turning the packet over in his hands. There was something about Melanie's ambition, her ability to transform the humblest of fruits and the simplest of treats into something extraordinary, that stirred a newfound respect within him.

"Melanie thinks of everything," Abby continued, her voice tinged with affectionate respect. "And I get to play with food all day. It's a win-win."

"Sounds like it," Lucas agreed, his thoughts already jumping ahead to how he could contribute to this blend of innovation and tradition. He felt a flicker of excitement at the prospect, a hopefulness he hadn't experienced in a long time.

Lucas followed the rhythmic clanking and whirring sounds until they brought him to the heart of Melanie's operation – the freeze-drying machines. They stood like silent sentinels, rows upon rows of stainless-steel promising alchemy. As he watched trays laden with vibrant strawberries, bananas, and an assortment of greens being slotted into the mechanical giants, Lucas felt a sense of wonder akin to witnessing a magic trick up close.

"Look at that," Lucas noted, pointing toward the glass, where he could see the moisture being drawn out from the produce. "It's like they're being tucked into bed for a long winter's nap, only to wake up still fresh."

The process was mesmerizing. Each tray held its own miniature ecosystem, soon to be stilled in time. The hum of the machines provided a bass line to the bustling melody of the warehouse, and as the fruits and vegetables surrendered their water content, they retained their shape and color, now locked in a state of suspended animation.

Lucas's attention then shifted to the employees who handled the preserved goods with care that bordered on reverence. A young man with deft fingers aligned the packets of freeze-dried raspberries into boxes labeled with precision, while a woman nearby inspected each bag of mixed veggies before sealing them with a vacuum sealer.

"Melanie doesn't compromise on details, does she?" Lucas mused aloud.

"Never," came the proud reply from Abigail. "Every package is a testament to her dedication. You can tell someone's soul by how they treat the little things."

Lucas picked up a packet of freeze-dried peaches, examining the label.

There was Melanie's touch – the font, a warm and inviting script; the colors, reminiscent of a sunset over the farm; and the slogan, 'Bite into Freshness Anytime, Anywhere.'

"Much like a well-loved recipe, it's not just about the ingredients but how you put them together," Lucas reflected.

"Exactly," agreed Abigail. "And Melanie's recipes are always spot-on."

Lucas followed the hum of machinery into the next chamber of the warehouse, where a man with a clipboard under his arm and an air of authority approached them. Jacob Sallinger's eyes were sharp, missing nothing as he moved through the plant, yet when they landed on Melanie, they softened just a hair before he schooled his features back to professional neutrality.

"Ah, you must be Lucas," Jacob said, extending a hand that Lucas shook, noting the firm grip of a man accustomed to hard work. "I'm Jacob Sallinger, the foreman here."

"Nice to meet you, Jacob," Lucas replied. "Melanie's been giving me the tour."

"Then you've seen just the tip of the iceberg," Jacob said with a chuckle. "Let me give you a rundown of how we keep this place ticking."

As they walked, Jacob gestured to various parts of the warehouse, detailing the daily dance of logistics with a practiced ease. "Coordinating with suppliers ensures we have a steady stream of top-quality produce—timing is everything. And then there's managing our distribution channels so that these beauties," he motioned toward a stack of neatly boxed products, "reach customers at peak freshness."

"Seems like a complex operation," Lucas observed.

"Complex, but rewarding," Jacob replied, pride evident in his tone. "Everyone here knows their part in the big picture."

They continued on, passing through the production floor with its freeze-drying units humming steadily. The air was cool and dry, filled with a sense of purpose. Then they stepped into the packaging department, where employees handled the products with care, ensuring each item was ready for its journey.

"Quality control is vital, as you can see," Jacob pointed out. "Melanie insists on it, and frankly, so do I."

"Attention to detail," Lucas mused.

"Exactly." Jacob nodded. "And once everything's packed, it's over to shipping." He led Lucas to a wide bay where boxes were being loaded onto trucks. "These will be all over the country by tomorrow."

"Remarkable," said Lucas, genuinely impressed. The scale of Melanie's operations was something to behold.

"Come on," Melanie interjected, a slight smile playing on her lips as she caught Lucas's eye. "There's more to see, and I've got some samples waiting for us that I think you'll appreciate."

Lucas trailed Melanie as they navigated through the maze of machinery and busy workers, the hum of productivity a constant backdrop to their tour. They approached a group of technicians huddled around a large console, their eyes fixed on a series of graphs and numbers flashing across the screen.

"Freeze-drying isn't just about preservation," Melanie explained. "It's about capturing the moment of perfect ripeness, locking in that flavor."

Lucas leaned in, observing the precision with which the technicians adjusted settings. "So, it's a race against time?"

"Exactly. And trends," she replied, gesturing toward the screens displaying market analysis data. "We have to innovate rapidly to stay ahead. Like these," she pointed to a graph highlighting a spike, "superfoods. A year ago, no one knew about freeze-dried goji berries. Now, they're everywhere."

"Timing is everything, then," Lucas mused.

"Timing and creativity," Melanie added, her eyes shining with the thrill of the challenge.

"Hey, Lucas, check this out!" An employee waved him over, a broad grin on his face. "Ever seen a strawberry get turned into a crispy chip before?"

"Can't say that I have," Lucas admitted.

"Melanie's brainchild. Kids love 'em—parents too, all natural, no additives."

"Brilliant," Lucas said after a crunch, the berry's essence bursting forth vividly. "Simple but innovative."

"Melanie's got a knack for it," another employee chimed in, packing boxes with practiced ease. "She's not just our boss, you know? She's one of us. Works as hard, if not harder. Makes you want to give it your all."

"Sounds like you're all invested in this place," Lucas observed, recognizing the sense of ownership in each team member's demeanor.

"Definitely! It's like we're all part of something big, something special," the employee said with conviction.

Melanie beamed at her team, clearly proud. Lucas could see the mutual respect flowing between her and her staff. The realization dawned on him that this venture was not just a business but a community. And in that moment, he felt an unexpected kinship with the people around him, a common thread of aspiration weaving them together.

Melanie led the way through a set of double doors, her stride confident as she pushed them open to reveal a room that contrasted sharply with the industrial backdrop they had just left. The tasting room was warmly lit and welcoming, with a long table at its center.

"Welcome to where magic happens," Melanie said, a playful glint in her green eyes. She motioned Lucas toward the array of colorful products spread out like an artist's palette across the sleek surface.

"Is this all freeze-dried?" Lucas asked, his gaze sweeping over the variety.

"Every bit of it," Melanie confirmed, picking up a packet of what appeared to be ice cream dots. "Try these."

Lucas watched as she popped a few into her mouth, her expression one of unabashed delight. Following suit, he was immediately taken aback by the taste.

"Whoa," he said, chuckling. "That's surprisingly good."

"Right?" Melanie laughed. "We're working on getting it into outdoor adventure stores. Imagine being able to have ice cream on a hiking trail."

He tried another sample, this time a piece of mango that melted back into its juicy state the moment it hit his palate. "The texture is remarkable. And the flavor—it's like eating a fresh mango."

"Exactly!" She looked pleased. "Freeze drying locks in the flavor. It's perfect for smoothies, baking, or even as a snack straight from the package. I've eaten more freeze-dried grapes than anyone should admit to."

They moved down the line, Melanie offering insights into potential recipes and pairings, her knowledge as deep as it was passionate. Lucas found himself drawn into her world, each bite a new discovery.

"Your creativity seems boundless," Lucas remarked, genuinely impressed. He watched her face light up with pride.

"Thank you, Lucas. It's necessary in this business to keep pushing boundaries." Melanie handed him a piece of freeze-dried pineapple. "And I love every minute of it."

"Your dedication is clear," Lucas said, his voice warm. "It's not just about running a successful business for you, is it?"

Melanie shook her head. "No, it's about creating something meaningful, something that adds a little joy to people's lives. Whether they're on a mountain top or in their own kitchen."

Lucas nodded, understanding dawning. This wasn't only about food. It was about connection, about crafting moments of happiness. And as they sampled and discussed, the pieces of a larger picture began to fall into place for him.

"Seeing all this," Lucas paused, gesturing around the room, "I'm beginning to see how much more there is to what you do. It's inspiring, Melanie."

She met his gaze squarely, a hint of vulnerability in her eyes. "I'm glad you think so," she said softly. "It means a lot to me."

In that space, surrounded by the fruits of Melanie's labor, Lucas felt an admiration for her that went beyond professional respect. There was a kindred spirit in her drive, her commitment to excellence—a mirror to his own aspirations.

Lucas stepped back from the tasting table, a thoughtful expression etching his face as he watched Melanie interact with her staff. She moved with a certainty that resonated deep within him—a mirror to his own confidence yet tinged with something new, something he was unaccustomed to feeling since his wife passed away: a sense of boundless potential.

"Melanie," Lucas began, his voice steady but imbued with newfound enthusiasm, "I've seen enough today to know that you're not just running a business here. You're nurturing a community, and what you're doing is extraordinary."

Melanie turned toward him, her green eyes reflecting a mixture of surprise and delight. "You really think so?"

"Absolutely." He took a step closer, and the din of the warehouse seemed to fade into the background. "I came here looking for a fresh start, a purpose. And I can't help but feel like what you've built here... it's more than I ever expected to find."

"Lucas," she said, stepping forward, "your support means everything. But this—" she gestured expansively, encompassing the hustle of the warehouse, "—this is just the beginning. There are challenges, yes, but the opportunities...they're endless."

"Then let's face those challenges together," he replied, conviction firm in his voice. Maybe he didn't know if he could ever love her, but he knew they would make good partners. "And let's seize those opportunities. I believe in what you're doing here, Melanie, and I want to be a part of it. Not just in business, but in every way that counts."

"Partners, then?" Melanie extended her hand, her grip firm and sure.

"Partners," Lucas confirmed, shaking her hand with equal vigor. He thought quickly they should be sealing their partnership with a kiss, but not yet. They weren't quite there, but he hoped with everything inside him they would be one day.

Chapter Five

Melanie led Lucas through the fields of her family farm. Despite the early hour, Lucas walked with a confident stride. His dark brown hair caught the light of the rising sun, and he took in the sprawling acres with an appreciative, if somewhat uncertain, eye.

"Joe will show you the ropes," Melanie said. "He's been the heart of this place for more than three decades."

Lucas nodded, his broad shoulders squared against the unfamiliar backdrop of rolling fields and the distant silhouette of tractors. He was a man more accustomed to boardroom battles than the quiet toil of farm life, yet there was a hopeful spark in his brown eyes—a silent promise to himself to embrace whatever came next.

As they approached a weathered barn, a figure emerged from the shadowy interior. Joe Digger, with his gray hair and steady brown gaze, extended a firm hand toward Lucas. The lines on Joe's face spoke of years under the sun and wind.

"Melanie tells me you're looking to start fresh," Joe said.

"Something like that," Lucas replied, shaking Joe's hand.

"Let me lay it out for you then," Joe began, gesturing for them to walk along as he talked. They moved past rows of crops, each one meticulously cared for, the result of unseen hands and tireless work. "You'll be overseeing all of this," he swept his arm across the expanse, "and more. Planting, harvesting, maintenance—"

"Animal care too?" Lucas interjected with genuine curiosity, keen to understand the full scope of his responsibilities.

"Of course, chickens, cows, horses, the whole lot," Joe confirmed with a nod. "It's hard work, but you've got a crew of ten to back you up. They know their stuff, been with me for years. They'll take your lead, as long as you show them you're willing to get your hands dirty alongside them."

Lucas absorbed Joe's words, the weight of responsibility settling on his shoulders. He liked the idea of tangible results from the work he did. He could plant and harvest a few months later. This was exactly what he'd been needing.

"Sounds like I have a lot to learn," Lucas admitted, the gleam in his eyes betraying his readiness for the challenge.

"Yep," Joe agreed. "But something tells me you're not the type to back down from a bit of hard work."

"Never have," Lucas said with a chuckle. "City skyscrapers or Missouri soil—it's all just another puzzle to solve, right?"

"Right you are," Melanie chimed in. She was excited that he seemed to be taking his role in her business seriously.

Lucas trailed behind Joe, his boots crunching on the gravel path that cut through the verdant fields of Melanie's farm.

"See there?" Joe said, pointing toward a distant barn. "That's where we keep the equipment. Over yonder" —he motioned to the south—"is prime grazing for the cattle."

Lucas nodded, committing every detail to memory, his mind buzzing with the magnitude of it all.

"Of course," Joe continued, his voice dropping a notch, "I won't be around to see it much longer."

"Is that so?" Lucas asked, a crease of concern forming between his brows. He certainly hoped the man would be around long enough to train him properly.

"Yep." Joe sucked in a breath, squinting up at the sky. "Been doing this for more years than I care to count. Time to hang up my hat soon—as soon as we find someone who can fill these boots."

The weight of those words settled on Lucas's shoulders like a winter coat, heavy and unexpected. Could he be the one? He glanced over at Melanie, whose eyes were trained on him.

"Big boots to fill," Lucas murmured, more to himself than anyone else.

"Sure are," Joe agreed, clapping a hand on his back. "But you'll have help. And time. Nothing happens overnight on a farm."

As they walked toward the first task of the day, Lucas's mind spun with what lay ahead. The familiar confidence that had propelled him through boardrooms felt strangely distant now, faced with the reality of dirt under his fingernails and the sun on his neck.

"Here we are," Joe announced, stopping beside a tractor that seemed to dwarf Lucas.

"Ever driven one of these?" Joe asked, a mischievous twinkle in his brown eyes.

"Can't say that I have," Lucas confessed, his voice edged with a laugh.

"Today's your lucky day then," Joe said with a grin.

Lucas climbed into the cab, the seat creaking beneath him. His hands hovered over the levers and buttons, a hesitant pianist before an unfamiliar concerto. Joe's instructions filtered through the open window, a lifeline thrown to a man adrift in uncharted waters.

"Easy does it," Joe encouraged as Lucas tentatively engaged the clutch. The tractor lurched forward.

"Look at you go!" Melanie called out from where she stood a safe distance away.

Lucas felt a smile tugging at his lips, despite the awkward jerks of the tractor as he navigated across the field. It was nothing like steering through the chaos of city traffic, but it was a start.

As the morning wore on, Lucas found himself immersed in the rhythm of the farm. Each task was a puzzle, each solution a small victory. The sweat on his brow, the earthy scent in the air, the satisfaction of movement and purpose—it was all so different, so real. Far from the abstract deals and digital figures of his past life.

"Doing good, city boy!" Joe hollered, his approval floating over the fields.

"Thanks, Joe," Lucas replied, his voice steady, his heart hopeful. This land, this work, was teaching him something new about life, about himself.

Melanie called that she'd see him at home later as she headed back toward the house and possibly to the plant. Lucas was unsure of her plans for the day, but he knew he was needed right where he was, learning to farm. If only his administrative assistant could see him now. She'd be laughing.

Lucas's grip tightened around the handle of the pitchfork as he plunged it into the hay, muscles that had never known farm work straining against the unaccustomed labor.

"Square bales! Not too tight, not too loose," Joe instructed from across the barn, watching Lucas attempt to bind the hay. "You'll get the hang of it."

"Square bales," Lucas repeated under his breath, determined to master this new art form. Back in New York, his challenges were about mergers, contracts, and navigating boardroom politics, not wrestling with twine and hay.

There was something undeniably gratifying about the results of his efforts here—the growing stack of neatly tied bales signified progress in a way that spreadsheets never could.

"New York City's got nothing on this, eh?" Joe remarked with a knowing chuckle.

"Definitely a different pace," Lucas admitted. He hadn't anticipated the weight of the bales, or the persistence needed to keep up with the crew. He had to show them he could be their leader.

Lucas gripped the wooden handle of the pitchfork, his palms already raw from the unaccustomed labor, yet he refused to let it show. He stabbed into the hay with newfound vigor, muscles protesting movements they had never before been tasked with.

"Like this," Joe's voice cut through his concentration. He demonstrated turning the hay with practiced ease. Lucas watched, committing the technique to memory.

"Thanks," he said, adjusting his grip.

"Everyone starts somewhere," Joe replied. "Don't worry, you'll get the hang of it."

"Maybe by next harvest," Lucas jested.

With each new task, Lucas felt the gap between his old life and his present reality widen. The physical demands of farm work were relentless, but there was an unexpected rhythm to the labor that lulled his mind.

"Hey, Lucas, can you help with the irrigation lines?" a worker called out, snapping him back to the present.

"Sure thing," he called back, setting aside the pitchfork. As he walked over, Lucas reminded himself that every question asked was knowledge gained. Fumbling with the unfamiliar fastenings, he glanced over at Joe for guidance.

"Pull here, then twist," Joe instructed, pointing to a section of the pipe.

"Got it," Lucas said, feeling a rush of accomplishment as the water began to flow smoothly once again.

"Lucas, you're doing fine," Joe assured him as they walked back to the farmhouse. "It's all about persistence and teamwork."

"Something tells me I'm going to learn a lot about both," Lucas replied.

Later, after supper, he stood at the kitchen window, looking out over what he'd done that day.

"Beautiful, isn't it?" Melanie said, her voice soft beside him.

"More than words can say," Lucas replied.

Before bed, Melanie went with him out to gather eggs, a task Lucas had watched but never attempted himself. Armed with a basket and an abundance of caution, he opened the gate and stepped inside. Chickens scattered in a flurry of feathers and indignant squawks, leaving Lucas to wonder if perhaps he'd missed a step in the process.

"Easy there, big guy," Melanie chuckled, her hand catching the door before it swung shut. "They're just chickens."

"Right, just chickens," he echoed, though his heart raced as if he'd faced down a boardroom of investors instead.

Squatting down, he reached for an egg nestled in the straw, his movements exaggeratedly gentle. The egg wobbled precariously before rolling from his grasp, shattering against the floor with an audible crack.

"Guess I'm already good at breaking them," Lucas quipped.

"Practice makes perfect," she assured him, her laughter mingling with the clucking of hens. "And we have plenty of eggs."

As the week unfolded, Lucas found himself moving from task to task, each one new and challenging in its own right. He wrestled with stubborn weeds that seemed to mock his urban upbringing. He fumbled with the knobs of the ancient tractor, earning a few teasing jibes from the crew, who took bets on how many tries it would take before he got the engine roaring to life.

"Third time's the charm," Lucas declared, finally coaxing the machine into a rumbling purr. His pride swelled at the small victory, a stark contrast to the world he knew, where success was measured in profits and power points.

With the setting sun casting long shadows once more, Lucas leaned against the fence, watching the cows amble toward the barn for milking. There was beauty in their unhurried pace, a lesson in patience and presence he was only beginning to understand. The simplicity of farm life wasn't just about the tasks or the landscape; it was a rhythm, a heartbeat that resonated deep within him, syncing with his own.

"Another day down," Melanie observed. "How are you holding up?"

"Better than I ever thought possible," Lucas admitted, his smile genuine. "I've made more mistakes today than in a whole year in New York, but somehow, it feels exactly right."

"Welcome to farm life, Lucas. It suits you," Melanie said.

Lucas's hands had grown accustomed to the grip of the hoe and the weight of the feed bags, a stark contrast to the smooth keys of a laptop and the leather-bound portfolios he once carried. He wiped the sweat from his brow as he surveyed the rows of freshly planted seedlings that stood in neat lines across the fertile soil. It was hard work, the kind that left you with an ache in your bones and satisfaction deep in your soul.

"Lucas," Melanie called from across the field, "look at this!" Her hand, smudged with dirt, cradled a tiny green shoot pushing its way through the earth.

"Would you look at that?" Lucas marveled, crouching beside her. "I can't believe I helped bring that little guy to life."

"Believe it," Melanie said with a smile. "You're a natural."

"Today was good," he told Melanie as they strolled toward the house.

"Every day you're here is good," she replied, her tone light but sincere.

"Melanie," Lucas began, stopping to face her, "I never thought I'd say this, but I think I'm starting to understand the appeal of this place. There's a rhythm here that makes sense to me now."

"It's not about understanding the land, Lucas. It's about feeling it. You're getting there."

That night, as he sat alone on the porch steps, Lucas reflected on the paths he had taken. Here, he found clarity in simplicity, purpose in toil, and joy in small victories. He was no longer the man who needed control of every situation; here, he was a student of life, and life was a generous teacher.

"Hey," Melanie's voice pulled him from his thoughts. She handed him a steaming mug of tea. "Thought you might like this."

"Thank you," Lucas accepted, wrapping his hands around the warmth.

"Anytime," she said, sitting beside him. They sipped in silence, the stars above bright and clear.

He was surprised at just how right it felt to sit beside her on the porch, looking out over the farm he'd worked all day. Perhaps this was where he was meant to be all along.

Chapter Six

L ucas settled into the rustic charm of the farmhouse, a warm plate of Melanie's homemade lasagna before him. The aroma of herbs and roasted tomatoes filled the dining room, mingling with the comfortable silence that wrapped around them like a cozy blanket. After a week that had pushed his limits, the quiet of the Missouri countryside felt like exactly what he needed in life.

Melanie shared a contented smile as she took a sip of her water. Lucas couldn't help but admire the way her slender frame perched at the edge of her chair, every bit the embodiment of success and determination he'd come to know so well.

"Thanks for helping teach me the ropes this week," Lucas said. "I never knew there was so much to learn about freeze-drying strawberries."

"Happy to share my knowledge," Melanie replied, her green eyes sparkling with amusement. "It beats doing it all alone."

A lull in the conversation opened up, and Melanie leaned back, gazing thoughtfully at a cabinet beside the fireplace. "You know, what I look forward to after long days like these are my puzzles." Her voice carried a hint of wistfulness, a rare vulnerability peeking through her usually composed exterior.

"Puzzles?" Lucas echoed, curious. He remembered a stack of colorful boxes tucked away on a shelf he'd glimpsed once before. And he'd helped her finish a puzzle on his first night there, but she hadn't said anything about them since.

"Jigsaw puzzles," Melanie clarified. "Something about piecing together those bits of color and shape—it's soothing, you know?"

Lucas's smile broadened. "Yeah, I get that. And working on that little one with you last time—that was fun."

"Little?" Melanie teased. "That was a five-hundred-piecer, Lucas. You're quite good at them."

"Ah, well," Lucas chuckled, his confidence never faltering, "I suppose I have a knack for figuring things out. It comes with the territory of starting over, doesn't it?"

"Yes, I guess it does," Melanie agreed.

Lucas and Melanie found comfort in the simple joys of their newfound friendship, unaware of just how perfectly they fit together.

Lucas rose from his seat, the remnants of their quiet dinner still lingering in the air. "Show me your collection," he said.

Melanie led him to a cozy corner of the living room where the shelves sagged under the weight of countless puzzle boxes, each emblazoned with images ranging from serene landscapes to abstract patterns. Her fingers danced over the cardboard edges as she considered her choices.

"Here," Melanie finally declared, pulling out a hefty box that depicted a sprawling tapestry of rolling hills and a kaleidoscope sunset. "This one's a good size— a thousand pieces."

"Looks like a worthy adversary," Lucas remarked.

They returned to the dining table, now cleared of plates and glasses, a blank canvas awaiting its masterpiece. The box opened with a soft sigh, releasing the scent of fresh cardboard and ink. Together, they tipped it sideways and let the sea of jigsaw pieces cascade onto the tabletop.

As they sifted through the chaos, arranging edge pieces and sorting by color, their movements created an easy rhythm. Melanie's slender fingers plucked a piece from the pile just as Lucas reached for it, and their hands brushed in passing.

"Sorry," Melanie said.

"No harm done," Lucas replied.

The puzzle began to take shape under their combined efforts, each piece a tiny triumph as it snapped into place.

Lucas watched as Melanie's red hair tumbled forward when she leaned in to examine a particularly stubborn section. There was a focus in her gaze that drew him in, an intensity that spoke of her passion for the things she loved. It was that same determination he suspected had propelled her business from humble beginnings to success.

"Got one!" Melanie exclaimed, fitting a piece into a stubborn gap, her face alight with satisfaction.

"Nice find," Lucas praised.

With a flick of her wrist, Melanie slid another piece into place, the satisfying click echoing in the spacious room. "You know," she said, eyes twinkling, "my grandmother and I used to spend hours on puzzles like these. She always said it was about the journey, not just the picture at the end."

"Sounds like a wise woman," Lucas responded, scanning the array of colors and shapes scattered across the table. "My favorite puzzle memory? The time I thought I had finished one, only to discover a piece missing. Turned out my dog had decided it looked tasty." He chuckled at the recollection, his shoulders relaxed despite the challenge before them.

Melanie laughed, the sound light and carefree. "Did you ever find it?"

"Two days later, under the couch, slightly...modified." His grin was infectious, and for a moment, they shared the humor of life's small surprises.

As the evening wore on, each piece they joined seemed to draw them closer, a silent testament to their growing connection. Melanie's hands moved with precision and grace, her fingers deftly picking out the correct pieces as if they called out to her. Lucas found himself admiring not just the way she bit her lip in concentration, but also her innate skill at discerning the intricate patterns within the chaos.

"Remarkable," he murmured, watching her work. The landscape before them was slowly coming alive, each section a testament to Melanie's keen intellect.

"Thanks," she said without looking up, fully absorbed. "My grandma always said I had an eye for these things."

"Your ability to see the big picture while still focusing on the small details is impressive," he complimented her, wondering if she'd realize he was talking about her business as well as the puzzle.

Melanie glanced up, a soft blush coloring her cheeks. "It's just a puzzle, Lucas."

"Maybe," he conceded with a thoughtful nod. "But it says a lot about you. And I have a feeling that's true for more than just puzzles."

Lucas watched Melanie lean across the table, her slender fingers deftly picking out a puzzle piece from the scattered mosaic of colors. The way she tilted her head, considering where it might fit in the grand scheme of the landscape they were piecing together, was a silent dance of concentration and grace. He found himself mesmerized by the focused furrow of her brow.

"Gotcha!" Melanie exclaimed triumphantly, snapping the piece into place. "That was hiding in plain sight!"

"Seems you're full of surprises," Lucas said. He picked up a piece with a swath of sunset sky on it, trying to match it to the emerging picture.

"Life's too short for predictability," she replied.

As they worked side by side, a comfortable rhythm established itself between them. Melanie's quick wit sparked bouts of laughter that echoed off the walls. Their conversation meandered through anecdotes of past puzzle conquests and gentle jibes about each other's strategies.

Amidst the laughter, Lucas caught himself stealing glances at Melanie. The way her red hair cascaded over her shoulder as she leaned forward, utterly engrossed in finding the next piece, struck him as singularly captivating.

"Lucas, wake up," Melanie's voice pulled him from his reverie, a hint of affectionate impatience in her tone.

"Right, sorry," he said, flashing her a sheepish grin. He placed his piece, feeling a small victory when the edges lined up perfectly against its neighbors.

Lucas reached for a piece, his hand hovering as he scanned the remaining gaps in the puzzle. "Gotcha," he muttered under his breath, slotting it into place with a satisfying click. He glanced up at Melanie, who had just completed a particularly tricky section of the landscape's horizon. Their eyes met, and without missing a beat, they exchanged high-fives, their palms meeting in a moment of shared success.

"Teamwork makes the dream work," Melanie quipped, a playful smile dancing on her lips as she nudged him lightly with her elbow.

"Is that your secret to running the farm so efficiently?" Lucas asked, his tone light but his curiosity genuine.

"Absolutely," she replied, her fiery hair cascading over one shoulder as she leaned forward to scrutinize the pieces. "But I have to admit, having a good partner helps."

They worked in silence for a few minutes as they tried to each find more pieces that would fit.

"Look at this," Melanie said, holding up two seemingly unrelated pieces. "You wouldn't think they'd go together, but—" With a gentle push, they clicked into place, completing another section of the rolling hills that spread across the puzzle.

"Sort of like us, huh?" Lucas ventured. "Different backgrounds, different skills, but somehow..."

"...somehow, we fit," Melanie finished for him, her gaze warm and thoughtful. "It's all about finding the right connection."

The edges of his mouth lifted into an appreciative smile. The puzzle did indeed reflect their budding relationship—two individuals learning to navigate the complexities of partnership, celebrating small victories, and facing challenges head-on, together.

"Who knew a jigsaw could be so philosophical?" he teased.

"Life's full of surprises, Lucas Barnett," Melanie said. "And maybe some of the best ones are hiding in plain sight, among a thousand scattered pieces waiting to be assembled."

As the final sections of the puzzle found their places, Lucas couldn't help but feel that the picture they were completing was more than just a game—it was a promising glimpse into a future they could build together, piece by piece.

Lucas picked up the final puzzle piece, its edges worn from being passed back and forth as they searched for its rightful place. Melanie watched him, her red hair cascading over her shoulders, a symbol of the patience and grace she'd brought to both the puzzle and to his life. With a playful flourish, he slotted the piece into the remaining gap, completing the intricate landscape that sprawled before them.

"Done!" Lucas exclaimed, raising his arms in victory.

"Finally!" Melanie's cheer mingled with his, her slender hands clapping in delight. They looked at each other, their eyes locking in a moment of shared triumph. She realized she'd never done a puzzle with someone who matched her skill quite so well. It was odd how very compatible they were, even though they'd only met less than a week before.

"Looks amazing, doesn't it?" Melanie's voice was soft but carried a twinge of pride.

"More than amazing," Lucas replied.

"Who would have thought," he mused aloud, "that two people could come together and make something so...perfect?"

"Perfect?" Melanie echoed. "Let's not jinx it. But I'll admit, it feels pretty close."

Lucas reached across the table, his hand hesitating for just a moment before finding Melanie's. Their fingers slid together effortlessly.

"Thank you," he said. "For sharing this...and for being here." And for so many other things he couldn't quite put into words. Being here with her was definitely the new beginning he needed.

"I can't remember the last time I enjoyed an evening like this so much," she admitted, her green eyes sparkling in the low light of the farmhouse.

He marveled at how natural this felt—holding Melanie's hand, sharing small victories, building something tangible and beautiful from a scattered array of pieces.

"Melanie," Lucas began, "I think we make a pretty good team."

Her lips curled into a smile. "I'd say more than pretty good," she teased lightly.

"Maybe we should tackle more puzzles together," Lucas suggested, his voice steady despite the fluttering in his chest.

"Maybe we should," Melanie agreed.

Lucas leaned in, the warmth of Melanie's hand still radiating through his. Her eyes, bright like embers in the soft farmhouse light, held a question that his heart answered without hesitation. His lips met hers in a comfortable kiss.

At first, it was gentle, a mere whisper of contact. It was the kind of kiss that said, "I see you," and "I am here" – simple yet profound. But as the seconds stretched on, the kiss deepened, growing more insistent as if drawn by a current neither of them could control.

Melanie's breath hitched. Lucas could feel the change, the way her surprise mirrored his own as passion took root where comfort had been. Their bodies edged closer, instinctively seeking the heat that bloomed between them. His fingers, once content to simply hold hers, now threaded through her long red hair, cradling her head with tenderness.

The world around them narrowed until there was nothing but the two of them. The puzzle lay forgotten, its picture complete, while they explored this new, uncharted connection that unfolded with every second their lips remained locked.

As Lucas finally drew back, he realized that life was painting a landscape more vivid and thrilling than any he could have envisioned.

In the quiet aftermath, they exchanged a look of mutual wonder, their kiss having opened a door they both hesitated to acknowledge was even there. Yet, as they sat in the afterglow, Melanie realized that what started as a shared triumph over a thousand-piece puzzle had blossomed into something infinitely more complex and beautiful.

Chapter Seven

Melanie sat at her desk, a fortress of papers standing tall before her. She sifted through invoices and order forms with the precision of a seasoned strategist, her green eyes scanning figures and forecasts that told the tale of her thriving freeze-drying business. She hated doing business on a Saturday afternoon, especially when she was so newly married, but Lucas was out meeting with the vet over one of the horses. She would work until she heard him return to the house.

Amidst the sea of documents, something unusual caught Melanie's attention—a book with a vibrant cover tucked away under a stack of supply lists. It was a marketing guide she didn't remember purchasing, its title embossed in bold, promising letters. Curiosity flickered in her mind like a spark threatening to ignite. She set aside her paperwork, reached for the book, and turned it over in her hands. She hadn't gone to college, but she learned as much as she could on her own. Perhaps she should lean a little more on Lucas's business acumen.

"Discover Your Business Potential: A Modern Approach to Marketing" read the title. With a mixture of skepticism and intrigue, Melanie flipped open the cover and began to peruse the pages. Paragraphs about market analysis, brand positioning, and consumer engagement leaped out at her, each concept resonating with an unexpected familiarity. It was as if the words were pieces of a jigsaw puzzle she'd been solving nightly, falling effortlessly into place. Now she remembered this book. She'd purchased it long before, and the housekeeper must have been working in her office and set it on her desk.

When she'd purchased it, it had made little sense, because she knew nothing of the finer points of business. Now that she looked at it again, it made sense to her, and she was thrilled.

As she delved deeper into the chapters, a revelation washed over her. She wasn't just comprehending the strategies; she was anticipating them, her mind racing ahead to the next point, the next tactic. It was thrilling, this sense of kinship with the subject matter. Marketing wasn't just a series of dry principles. It was something she not only understood but excelled at.

Her heart began to race with the budding recognition of her own capabilities. How many ideas had she already implemented without even realizing they were textbook tactics? The seasonal campaigns, the community events, the personal touches in customer service—all facets of an innate talent she hadn't known she possessed.

The potential of what this meant for her business sent a wave of excitement coursing through her veins. She could see it now, the path unfurling before her, ripe with opportunity.

Melanie leaned back in her chair, the marketing book clutched in her hands like a treasure chest of possibilities. A smile tugged at the corners of her mouth, born of a confidence that felt both old and new.

With a sense of purpose, Melanie strode toward the barn, the marketing book snug under her arm. The rhythmic sound of Lucas's work with the animals punctuated the air, and she found herself moving to its comforting beat.

Lucas was busy raking fresh straw into the stalls, his broad shoulders flexing with each movement. He didn't notice her immediately, so engrossed was he in his task, which allowed Melanie a moment to admire the steadfast man who had come to share in her world.

"Lucas," she called out gently.

He turned toward her voice, his face breaking into a warm smile that reached his eyes and crinkled the corners. "Hey there, Mel," Lucas greeted, leaning his weight onto the rake. "What brings you out to my humble abode?"

Melanie's own smile mirrored his as she closed the distance between them. The excitement within her bubbled up again, like champagne fizzing eagerly to escape the bottle. She could hardly contain the news that felt like it would change everything.

"I've just had the most amazing realization," she began, her voice alive with enthusiasm. She took a breath, grounding herself in the moment before sharing her vision. "I've been reading this marketing book, and Lucas, it's like I've discovered a hidden part of myself." Her hands animatedly gestured to the book, as if it were a sacred text containing all the secrets of their success yet to come.

Lucas's brows rose, his interest piqued by her fervor. "Oh yeah?" he said, straightening up, the rake momentarily forgotten. "Tell me more about this epiphany of yours."

Melanie opened the book to a dog-eared page, pointing to a passage that had particularly inspired her. "It's all here—how to connect with customers, build our brand, create a message that resonates. I've been doing some of these things instinctively, but now I see how we can amplify it, and make it intentional. There's so much potential for the business, and I think I can lead us there." When he simply grinned, she continued. "Most companies who work with freeze-dried food focus their marketing on people who think the world is ending—preppers. But I immediately put my focus on the busy moms. I see my ideal client as a mom who finds herself as the primary breadwinner who has a couple of kids, maybe one is autistic, and a husband who has health issues and can't work. But she's still the one who's trying to figure out all the meals because she's the mom, and it's expected of her, even though she's the only one working. Does that make sense?"

Her words tumbled out in a rush, each one infused with the certainty that they were on the cusp of something grand. As she spoke,

Melanie watched Lucas absorb her passion, and saw the flicker of recognition in his eyes that mirrored her own determination.

He nodded. "Ramp up our marketing, huh?" Lucas said thoughtfully, a hint of admiration coloring his tone. "That sounds like an adventure. And if anyone can take us to the next level, it's you, Melanie." He didn't mention the marketing courses he'd taken in college as part of his MBA. It would be better if she figured things out on her own.

Lucas folded his arms, leaning against the wooden frame of the barn door. A soft smile played on his lips as he watched Melanie's animated gestures, her hands painting the future in broad, bold strokes. "You have an amazing head for business," he said, his voice a low timbre that carried the weight of his conviction. "This is your moment, Mel. Seize it."

With a nod, Melanie stepped closer, her hand finding his. Their fingers intertwined, a silent promise of partnership and support.

"Thank you, Lucas," she whispered, her voice catching with emotion. "With you by my side, I feel like anything is possible."

"Because it is," he replied, squeezing her hand gently before letting go.

"Would you mind if I bounced some ideas off of you?" she asked softly.

He smiled. "I'll help in any way I can." He was surprised at just how much he enjoyed watching her mind work as she came up with new ideas. She was worming her way into his heart whether he liked it or not.

Melanie turned, her stride purposeful as she made her way back to her office. She rolled up her sleeves, ready to dive into the world of marketing with fresh eyes and renewed vigor. The whiteboard loomed large against the far wall, a blank canvas awaiting her ideas.

Pulling a marker from the tray, she uncapped it with a satisfying click. Her thoughts tumbled onto the board in a flurry of words and sketches. "Social media," she wrote, underlining it twice for emphasis. A web of lines connected to new phrases: "Engaging content" and "Brand ambassadors."

She paused. "Local collaborations," she mused aloud. Her mind raced with potential: co-branded products, cross-promotions, and events that could weave the fabric of the community tighter around her burgeoning brand.

"Targeted ads," she added.

As the whiteboard filled, a sense of accomplishment swelled within her. This wasn't just a plan. It was a declaration of intent, a map leading toward a future ripe with success and satisfaction.

"All right, Melanie," she said to herself, a determined glint in her eye, "Let's make some magic happen."

Moving to her desk, Melanie's fingers danced across the keyboard with a rhythmic clatter, each tap a step closer to understanding her clientele. Glancing at the screen, she scrutinized the survey questions she'd formulated, each one crafted to peel back the layers of her customers' desires and preferences. With a click that sent the digital questionnaire flying through cyberspace, she leaned back in her chair, ready for the answers to her questionnaire to come back to her.

"Know your audience," she whispered to herself. Her inbox soon buzzed with incoming responses, and Melanie poured over every word, every suggestion, drawing patterns from their collective voices. She noted the enthusiasm for organic ingredients, the desire for more savory options, and the clamor for eco-friendly packaging.

"Tailoring," she mused, scribbling notes on a fresh page in her notebook. "Customize the experience." It was like putting together a jigsaw puzzle, finding where each unique piece fit into the grand design of her business.

With a treasure trove of insights now at her fingertips, Melanie cleared a space at the center of her crowded desk and unfurled a large sheet of paper. The white expanse beckoned, inviting her to map out the terrain of her ambitions. She began with broad strokes, outlining her goals with certainty—increased sales, expanded reach, deeper community connection. These were the pillars upon which she would build her temple of success.

"Step by step," she reminded herself, allocating funds with precision as she set the budget. Digital ads, influencer partnerships, print materials—each line item was allocated with care, balancing cost against potential return. It was a high-stakes balancing act, but Melanie felt the steadiness of a seasoned acrobat.

"Target audiences," she continued, segmenting her market with an analytical eye. Young professionals, health-conscious parents, culinary adventurers—they would all find something in her freeze-dried delights. And her key messages? They practically wrote themselves: "Indulge guilt-free," "Farm-fresh flavor anytime," "Sustainability never tasted so good."

Checking her watch, Melanie realized hours had slipped by unnoticed. A sense of pride swelled within her, not just for the strategy taking shape before her, but for the journey it represented—a path paved with resilience, creativity, and the joy of discovery.

"Here goes nothing," Melanie said, a confident smile playing on her lips. She was ready to breathe life into these pages, to turn theory into action.

Melanie strode into the barn, her boots clicking against the wooden floorboards with purpose. In her hand, she clutched the marketing plan, its pages brimming with notes and ideas. Lucas was there, as he always seemed to be, a calming presence among the soft sounds of the animals. His hands worked methodically, distributing feed, but his eyes found hers with an easy familiarity that managed to send a thrill down Melanie's spine.

"Hey," she said, her voice echoing slightly in the spacious barn. "Got a minute?"

"Always for you," Lucas replied, wiping his hands on his jeans before taking the papers she offered. He scanned them, his brow furrowing in concentration.

"Looks like you've got a solid start here," he observed, pointing to a section on social media outreach. "But have you considered a more visual approach? Maybe a series of videos showcasing the farm-to-table process?"

Melanie's eyes lit up. "That's brilliant. It would give a personal touch, make the customers feel connected to where their food comes from."

They moved to a hay bale and spread out the documents between them. Idea after idea sparked as they bounced thoughts back and forth, the energy palpable. They were two halves of a whole, fitting seamlessly together in business as in life.

"Okay, so we'll do a test shoot next week," Melanie decided, scribbling another note.

The following days were a whirlwind of activity. Melanie's office became mission control, her team gathered around the whiteboard that now displayed a mind map of creativity and deadlines. Her fingers danced across her laptop keyboard, responding to emails, scheduling posts, and confirming collaborations.

"Let's make sure these ads really pop," Melanie directed, leaning over the shoulder of her graphic designer, who was manipulating images with deft clicks. "Our products are vibrant and full of life, and that's exactly how they should look."

"Got it, Mel," came the enthusiastic response.

In tandem, Melanie coordinated with local businesses, securing partnerships that would introduce her freeze-dried products to new audiences.

"Check this out," her social media manager called. On the screen was a preview of the first video installment—a charming, sunlit journey through the farm, ending with the tagline "Savor the Simple" fading onto the screen.

"Perfect," Melanie breathed out. She could almost taste the success that awaited them, as tangible as the sweet strawberries they freeze-dried at the peak of ripeness.

"Looks like we're ready to launch," Lucas said, coming up behind her and placing a supportive hand on her shoulder.

"Ready when you are," she affirmed.

THREE WEEKS LATER, Melanie surveyed the latest sales reports. Figures danced merrily across her screen, each one a testament to the traction their marketing efforts were gaining. Orders were pouring in like rain during springtime, and social media was abuzz with glowing reviews and customer testimonials.

"Have you seen this, Lucas?" Melanie called out. She spun around in her chair to face him, her eyes sparkling with the kind of fervor that only a well-earned triumph could ignite.

Lucas leaned against the doorframe, arms folded, a proud smile playing on his lips. "I heard the team cheering from the barn," he said, pushing off from the wood with a casual grace. "That can only mean good news."

"Good news indeed!" she exclaimed. The screen in front of her displayed a graph, its line ascending sharply, mirroring the lift in her spirits. "Our sales have doubled since last month, and people are loving the new ad campaign." She gestured toward the computer.

He stepped forward, his gaze following the trajectory of her gesture. "Mel, this is incredible. You've outdone yourself," he praised.

"Lucas, with results like these," she began, "I think we're at a point where we need someone to take the reins of our marketing full-time.

Someone who understands our mission and cares about this business as much as I do."

She paused, searching his face before continuing, "What would you say to being our marketing director?"

The question hung between them, charged with potential and promise. Lucas's eyes met hers, a mixture of surprise and humility flickering within their depths. He ran a hand through his dark hair, considering the weight of her proposal.

"Me?" he asked, almost rhetorically. "I came here looking for a fresh start, something meaningful. Working alongside you, Mel, I've found that—and more. I'd be honored to help lead us into the next chapter."

"I guess that means I need to find a new manager for the farm...though I'm glad you started here, learning every aspect of the business." She leaned into him. "I wasn't expecting to marry a man who was so good at business."

He grinned. "That's what happens with an MBA."

"Then it's settled," she declared. "Welcome aboard, Director Barnett."

"As long as I'm allowed to keep working on the farm," Lucas said, "I can dive head first into marketing, but I still want to keep my boots dirty out there with Joe."

Melanie nodded, her red hair catching the sunlight that streamed through the open door. "Exactly. You've got a knack for this, Lucas. But I still want you to understand the farming side of the business."

A slow smile spread across his face, the decision crystallizing in his mind as clearly as the view of from the farmhouse on a cloudless day. Lucas could see it now—the balance of contributing to business growth without losing touch with the earthy roots that grounded him.

Melanie's grin mirrored his own, a reflection of shared contentment and anticipation. She reached across the desk, her slender fingers closing around his calloused hand. "We're going to make a great team, Lucas. Not just for the business, but for each other."

Lucas squeezed her hand in affirmation, warmth flooding through him. This was more than a job offer; it was a blend of her dreams and his desire for purpose. Together, they were sowing the seeds of success that would grow alongside the crops and cattle, nurtured by their joint passion and care.

"Let's do it, then," he said, his voice tinged with excitement. "Let's take this business—and our life—to places we've only imagined." He pulled her into his arms and held her close, thinking about how she had wormed her way into his heart. He almost felt guilty for having feelings for her, but he refused. No, they were married, and this was his new start.

Chapter Eight

They'd been married for eight weeks and were both deeply embroiled in their work when Lucas realized they needed some time together without work. They both enjoyed what they did, but they needed to have some time away as a couple.

As he fed the chickens that morning, he decided they needed a weekend away from work, and he was going to do whatever it took to make it happen.

He went into the house for breakfast and saw that Melanie already had it on the table. He was always amazed at how she did all the cooking with her busy workload and never asked him for help. He knew it was a lot for one person, but he also knew they were often eating a packaged meal that she'd simply added water to. She used her electric kettle like other women used a slow cooker or Instant Pot.

Breakfast that morning was scrambled eggs with bacon and cheese mixed right in, and they were delicious. As he took a sip of his morning coffee, he said, "We need a weekend away."

Her eyes widened. "It's the middle of growing and harvest season. I could spare a weekend in..." She picked up her phone and scrolled through her online calendar. "Late November or early December."

He sighed. "I was thinking more about leaving on Friday night and coming back on Sunday evening."

"This week?" she asked, her eyes wide in shock. "I can't possibly go anywhere this week."

"Can't Jacob and Abigail pick up your slack for one weekend?" he asked. They'd rarely kissed and never made love. It was time for them to do both.

"I guess they can, but it's still so quick..."

"Ocean? Mountains?" he asked.

"I've never seen an ocean. I was born and raised right here. My parents died while I was young, so my grandmother raised me..."

"Ocean it is. Not New York. West coast?"

"I don't know that we can do this so quickly."

"You don't usually work on weekends. Why would it be a problem?"

She sighed. "I guess I can call Jacob and Abigail and see what they think. It feels wrong just taking off though..."

MELANIE FELT THE REASSURING warmth of Lucas's hand envelop hers as they strolled across the expanse of the farm. She glanced at him, taking in his dark hair that caught the sunlight, and the lines around his eyes that spoke of smiles and a life rich with experience.

"The tomatoes are just about ripe for picking," Lucas remarked.

She nodded. It had been over three weeks since she'd last inspected the crops herself. The realization struck her. Melanie had become a bystander on her own land, yet there wasn't a trace of anxiety within her. Instead, she found a profound trust in Lucas, in his ability to manage the very heart of her world outside the plant's steel walls.

"Joe says we'll have a bumper crop this year," she replied.

"Doesn't surprise me with the way you've been running things. You've got a knack for growth, Melanie. More than just these crops." Lucas squeezed her hand slightly.

She smiled, the edges of caution that once defined her softening in his presence. As they paused by the edge of a field, Melanie looked up at him, her green eyes reflecting the vast sky above, clear and open.

"Jacob and Abigail, they've agreed to handle everything next weekend," she said, a flutter of excitement lining her words. There was something liberating about letting go, even if just for a brief while.

"Really?" Lucas's eyebrows raised, a spark of delight in his gaze. "You mean I'll have you all to myself without worries about the farm?"

"Seems like it." She couldn't help but mirror his smile. "I think they know how important this step is for us...for me."

"Then we'll make the most of it," he assured her.

As they resumed their walk, the shadows grew longer, stretching across the fields like fingers reaching for tomorrow. Melanie's heart danced to the thought of stepping away from the daily grind, entrusting her life's work into capable hands. For the first time in a long while, she embraced the idea of simply living in the moment.

"Mel," Lucas began, his voice threading through the soft rustling of the cornstalks. "You remember that musical you mentioned? The one you've always wanted to see but never had the chance?"

She turned toward him, her heart catching on an updraft of hope. "*Wicked*?" Her word hung between them, a single note waiting to harmonize with his next.

His grin was like the break of dawn over the horizon, warm and illuminating. "Exactly. I thought that's what we could do next weekend. I got us tickets for Saturday night in Portland."

"Portland?" The word echoed within her, a pebble dropped into the still waters of her routine life, sending ripples outward. Excitement surged. "Seriously?"

"First-row balcony," he added, as though unveiling the final piece of a cherished puzzle.

"Lucas, that's...that's amazing!" Her laughter bubbled up, airy and effervescent, yet a shadow of concern swiftly followed, tempering her joy. She bit her lip, contemplating the reality beyond the farm's boundaries. "But leaving the farm—even with Jacob and Abigail stepping in—I haven't been away since..."

"Since you've made this place your world," he finished gently.

Lucas reached out, his hand enveloping hers once more, grounding her amidst the whirlwind of emotions.

"Trust me, everything will be fine here," he said. "And just think about how magical the night will be—just you, me, and a little bit of Broadway magic."

"Magical," she repeated, allowing the simplicity of the idea to sink in. With Lucas, even the impossible seemed within reach. Maybe it was time to let go of her apprehensions and step out into the wider world, to allow herself the chance to be swept away by something extraordinary.

"Okay," Melanie breathed out. "Portland, here we come."

FRIDAY CAME FASTER than she anticipated. Standing in line at Lambert International Airport in St. Louis, Melanie fidgeted with the strap of her carry-on bag. Lucas's hand found the small of her back, a comforting presence that slowed her racing heart.

"First class?" she asked, eyes wide as he handed her the boarding pass.

"Nothing but the best," Lucas replied with a wink. It was his unspoken way of saying she deserved this break, this indulgence. The edges of her lips curved upwards, the very thought of leaning back in the spacious seats enough to make her feel light.

"Thank you," she whispered, leaning into his side. First class was a luxury she rarely afforded herself, too caught up in the practicalities of running a business. Yet here she was, about to soar above the clouds with the man who made her feel grounded.

"Come on," he urged gently. "Let's start this adventure right."

As they settled into the plush seats, Lucas's hand enveloped hers, a silent promise of support and shared excitement. Her worries about the farm began to fade, overshadowed by the anticipation of the weekend ahead.

"Portland won't know what hit it," Melanie said.

"Neither will we," Lucas chuckled, his thumb tracing circles on her palm. With Lucas by her side, Melanie felt confident that happiness wasn't just a fleeting moment, but a journey they were embarking on together.

THE PORTLAND SKYLINE welcomed them with its twinkling lights as the taxi weaved through the city, a stark contrast to the sprawling fields they had left behind. Melanie pressed her nose against the cool glass, watching the blur of storefronts and street lamps, soaking in the urban energy that was so different from her daily life.

"Here we are," Lucas announced as the car rolled to a stop in front of The Heathman Hotel, its grand façade oozing luxury.

Melanie's eyes widened at the sight, the hotel's posh exterior promising an opulence she didn't often indulge in. Stepping out of the taxi, she felt the crisp evening air brush against her skin, sending a shiver of excitement down her spine.

Lucas took care of the bags, his easy confidence reassuring Melanie as they approached the polished reception desk. She expected him to ask for two keys but watched in mute surprise as he pocketed a single gold card.

"Only one room?" she questioned, her voice a mix of curiosity and a flutter of something else she couldn't quite pin down.

"Hope that's okay with you," Lucas said, his eyes searching hers. "I thought...well, I just thought it would be nicer."

"Definitely nicer," Melanie agreed, the corners of her mouth curving into a smile that reflected her growing trust in this man who continued to surprise her.

They took the elevator to the top floor, and they stepped out into a quiet hallway. As Lucas led the way, Melanie found herself anticipating the view from their room, imagining the city laid out before them like a canvas of possibilities.

Dinner was a melody of flavors and laughter at a quaint bistro tucked away in a cobblestone alley, Lucas's choice proving impeccable. They savored each course, from the delicate appetizer to the rich, decadent dessert, paired with a wine that danced on the tongue.

"Did you enjoy that?" Lucas asked as they emerged back onto the lively streets.

"Every bite," Melanie admitted, feeling the edges of her old caution melting away in the warmth of his company. "My brain is already trying to come up with a way to imitate that cheesecake in freeze-dried form. I'm probably crazy, but that raspberry cheesecake flavor is still lingering on my tongue. I have to try."

He grinned, impressed that it was the first time she'd mentioned the business since they had arrived at the airport in St. Louis. Perhaps she was enjoying her time away. He hoped so.

They meandered back to the hotel, hand in hand, sharing stories and chuckles that bounced off the buildings around them. The night was alive with the sounds of the city, but all Melanie could hear was the steady rhythm of her heartbeat.

"Look at you, all carefree," Lucas observed, his voice soft with affection.

"Is it that obvious?" Melanie teased, though she knew he was right. This was the first time he'd seen her without the weight of the farm on her shoulders, the first time she truly allowed herself to live in the moment. And not just the first time since they'd married. The first time in the ten years since her grandmother had died.

"Completely," he confirmed, squeezing her hand gently. "It suits you."

As they reached the lobby of The Heathman, Melanie realized that she hadn't thought about the farm or her responsibilities since they'd landed other than the brief thought about imitating the cheesecake.

Here, under the gentle glow of chandeliers and Lucas's gaze, she was simply Melanie—alive, hopeful, and falling a little bit more for the man by her side.

The door clicked shut behind them, the sound a clear, definitive marker of privacy. Melanie leaned against the polished wood, her eyes never leaving Lucas as he turned back to face her, his hair slightly tousled from the evening breeze. The way he looked at her made her feel like she was the only person in the world that mattered.

"Melanie," he breathed out her name, and it felt like a caress against her skin, warm and promising. He took a step toward her, closing the distance with an ease that spoke of his innate confidence. She could see it, the gentle assertion in his stride, the underlying strength in his broad shoulders, but it wasn't overpowering. It was protective, encompassing, and deeply reassuring.

She pushed away from the door and met him halfway. When their fingers intertwined, there was a surge of electricity that seemed to pulse through her veins, anchoring her to this moment, to him.

"Lucas," she replied, her voice a whisper of excitement and a tremor of newness. She had not anticipated this moment when they first agreed to come here, but standing before him now, she couldn't imagine it unfolding any other way.

He drew her closer, and the touch of his lips was soft against hers, a tentative question that she answered by deepening the kiss, encouraging him with the parting of her lips. His response was immediate, passionate yet considerate, as though each movement was a word in a conversation only they understood.

Their bodies pressed together, heat building between them—a contrast to the cool sheets that would soon envelop them. With each layer of clothing that fell to the floor, Melanie felt a piece of her guard slip away, revealing a vulnerability she only trusted with Lucas.

In the dimly lit room, they explored the newfound contours and textures of each other's skin, mapping routes of pleasure with tender curiosity. Lucas was attentive, his touches imbued with a desire to learn every reaction, every sigh that escaped her lips.

He lowered her to the bed, happy to be away from the world that demanded so much of them. Her slender frame fit perfectly against his, her red hair a fiery cascade over the white pillowcase. As they moved together, everything seemed right with the world. Melanie felt as if she was where she needed to be.

"Are you okay?" Lucas's voice was low, tinged with concern as he paused, searching her face for any hint of discomfort.

"Yes," she assured him, wrapping her arms around his neck, pulling him back down to reaffirm her consent, her desire. "More than okay."

His movements resumed, confident but unhurried, as if time itself had agreed to slow down for them. With every gentle thrust, every shared breath, Melanie found herself drifting further from the woman who needed to control every aspect of her life. Here, in Lucas's embrace, she could let go, trust, and simply feel.

And when the crescendo of their union peaked, it resonated deep within her. There was no grand declaration, no need for words, just two hearts beating as one, finding solace and love in the quiet afterglow.

As they lay there, limbs entangled, Melanie felt as if this trip was the defining moment in her relationship with Lucas. If he could talk her into leaving her business for an entire weekend, she was sure he could do anything.

Chapter Nine

The morning sun filtered through the sheer curtains, casting a warm glow on the entangled sheets where Melanie lay, light and shadow playing over her bare skin. She stirred awake, her eyes fluttering open to find Lucas's steady gaze upon her. The remnants of her initial shyness crept up her cheeks as she became acutely aware of her nakedness in his presence.

"Good morning," he said, his voice a soft rumble.

"Morning," she whispered back, the curve of her lips tentative but genuine, her hair a fiery cascade across the pillow.

Lucas reached out, brushing a stray lock of her red hair behind her ear. His hair was tousled from sleep, yet he carried an air of control that was both comforting and exciting to Melanie. The atmosphere between them was charged with an intimacy that only seemed to grow with each passing moment.

With a gentle pull, he drew her closer, and the world outside their cocoon ceased to exist. Their kisses deepened, and Melanie's shyness evaporated like dew beneath the rising sun. They moved together in a rhythm as natural as the tide, rediscovering each other with a passion that left no room for hesitation. In those moments, Melanie forgot to be anything but wholly present, lost in the sensation and the undeniable connection she felt with Lucas.

Later, as they lay content in the afterglow, Lucas propped himself up on one elbow and looked down at her with a playful glint in his eye. "How about we rent a car and drive to the beach today?" he suggested.

Melanie considered it, the thought of the ocean's expanse and the feel of sand between her toes momentarily enticing. Yet as she glanced around the room, at the haven they had created, she realized she wasn't ready to leave just yet. There was something so liberating about being here with Lucas, away from the responsibilities of her burgeoning business and the vastness of her grandmother's farm.

"Actually," she began, a smile tugging at the corners of her mouth, "I think I'd prefer to stay in." Her voice was confident, sure of what she wanted, and Lucas nodded in agreement, clearly pleased with her decision.

"Room service it is, then," he concurred, reaching for the phone on the bedside table. His voice was filled with warmth as he ordered an array of breakfast delights—a feast fit for their private world.

As they waited, wrapped in each other's arms and bathed in the soft light of the morning, Melanie couldn't help but feel hopeful. Here in Portland, with Lucas, she found a happiness that was both new and exhilarating. She allowed herself to revel in the simple pleasure of spending time with him and him alone.

Time slipped through their fingers as they talked, ate, and made love some more. Lucas and Melanie lingered in the cocoon they had woven for themselves, a world that began and ended with the boundaries of the four walls enclosing them. The air was rich with the scent of their morning feast, now just a memory, and the echoes of laughter that had danced between them.

Melanie leaned against the windowpane, her red hair catching the fading light, watching the city below thrumming with life. Her body hummed with anticipation for the evening's entertainment, a musical she had dreamt of seeing since she'd first heard its enchanting score. Yet as she turned to look at Lucas, reclining with casual elegance on the plush sofa, her heart swelled with a longing that tethered her firmly to the spot.

"Can you believe it's nearly five already?" she said, her voice tinged with both excitement and a hint of regret. The thought of leaving this private sanctuary pained her, even if it was for something she eagerly awaited.

Lucas stood and crossed the room to where she was perched, his movements smooth and assured. He wrapped an arm around her slender waist and pulled her close, pressing a tender kiss to her forehead. "The show will be fantastic," he promised, "but these moments with you? They're irreplaceable."

At the restaurant, the atmosphere crackled with the energy of Portland's dining elite. They were seated at a table with crisp linens and gleaming silverware, a stark contrast to the informal meals they had shared back on Melanie's farm. Before them sat two perfectly seared steaks, aromatic and inviting.

"Isn't it strange?" Melanie mused aloud, slicing into the succulent meat. "Usually, when I'm out eating something delicious like this, part of my mind is dissecting the flavors, trying to figure out how I can recreate it later." She took a bite, savoring the burst of rich taste, and smiled at Lucas across the table.

"But tonight," she continued, a playful glint in her eye, "I don't want to think about recipes or freeze-drying techniques. Tonight, I just want to enjoy the food... to enjoy the here and now, with you."

Lucas raised his glass to her in a silent toast, admiration lighting his eyes. "Here's to new experiences, Mel. To us being present and finding joy in every moment."

As they dined, the conversation flowed as smoothly as the wine, and Melanie found herself lost in the depth of Lucas's gaze. With each passing minute, she realized that while the allure of the show was strong, the pull of this man—his presence, his warmth—was something far more potent, something not even the grandest stage could rival.

The yellow taxi melded with the stream of traffic as it carried Lucas and Melanie away from the restaurant. They sat close in the backseat, her hand finding his whenever the car jostled over a pothole or took a sharp turn. Outside, the neon glow of billboards and streetlights painted the dusk with strokes of vibrant color.

"Can't believe we're actually going," Melanie said, her voice threaded with excitement as the theater's marquee came into view. She leaned forward as if the proximity could somehow bring the moment to her faster.

"Believe it," Lucas replied. He paid the cab fare, and they stepped out onto the bustling sidewalk. The air was alive with the sounds of chatter and laughter, the mingling scents of pretzels and hot dogs wafting from nearby stands.

Melanie didn't notice. Her gaze was fixed on the entrance of the theater, on the posters that heralded the night's performance. Lucas watched her face light up, memorizing the way her green eyes sparkled under the marquee lights, the slight parting of her lips that betrayed her awe. He'd seen the show before, but this time, he knew, would be different because she was there beside him, living it for the first time.

As they made their way inside, found their seats, and settled in, the anticipation in the auditorium was palpable. The murmur of the crowd hushed to a whisper as the lights dimmed, signaling the beginning of the musical. Melanie shifted to the edge of her seat. The energy emanating from her was infectious, and he couldn't help but smile.

The orchestra struck the opening chord, and the stage came alive. Lucas glanced over at Melanie, observing the play of emotions crossing her face—surprise, delight, wonder—as the story unfolded before them. His own enjoyment of the musical was heightened by her reactions; every gasp, every chuckle, every tear that shimmered in her eye was a note in the melody of her experience.

And as the first act progressed, Lucas found himself less and less concerned with the performers on stage. Melanie was his focus. Her enthusiasm was a balm to the parts of him that had been too long shrouded in solitude. In her presence, he felt something awaken—a hope that perhaps starting over wasn't just about new places, but new people who made you see the familiar with fresh eyes.

As the house lights gently brightened, signaling intermission, Melanie unfolded from her seat like a flower greeting the morning sun. She stretched her arms high above her head, working out the kinks that had settled during her enraptured stillness. Lucas watched her with tender amusement, noting the way she seemed to sway slightly, as if reluctant to detach herself from the enchantment of the first act.

"Better?" he asked, his voice low and warm.

"Much," Melanie replied, though her eyes darted back to the stage, a silent vow to return to its magic as quickly as possible. Lucas recognized the fervor in her gaze—it was the same unspoken longing he'd come to know well, the hunger for life's next grand movement.

"I'll grab us some drinks," he said, standing and brushing past her knees. "Stay put. I won't be long."

"Thank you, Lucas," she said, but her voice was distant, lost already in thoughts of what awaited behind the curtain. She knew she should have offered to go with him, but she was worried she would miss even a second of the musical.

Lucas made his way up the aisle, navigating through the sea of theatergoers stretching their legs and chatting animatedly about the performance. At the concession stand, he ordered two drinks.

As he returned, the woman seated on his other side caught his eye—a kind-faced matron with silver streaks in her hair. Her smile held a touch of knowing as she leaned towards him just enough to be heard over the hum of intermission conversations.

"Excuse me," she said, "but you two must be newlyweds, right?"

Lucas paused, the corners of his mouth lifting into a half-smile. "What makes you say that?"

"Oh, it's obvious!" The woman's laugh was soft and pleasant. "The way you watch her, it's not with the casual interest of someone who has seen it all before. No, you look at her as if rediscovering the world—through her. It's quite sweet, truly."

Lucas chuckled, a sound that rumbled deep in his chest, filled with both pride and a newfound joy. "Well, we've been married six weeks. I guess that's still newlywed, isn't it?"

"I knew it," the woman mused, nodding sagely. "You two are going to be very happy together. I can feel it. Cherish these moments. They're precious."

"Yes, they are," Lucas agreed, his voice threaded with the weight of his intentions and the brightness of the future he hoped to build.

Returning to Melanie with the drinks in hand, he found her still standing, a sentinel of anticipation, ready to dive back into the story. He handed her a glass, and their fingers brushed—a simple touch that spoke volumes, promising more than any vow could.

"Cheers," Lucas said, raising his glass, to which Melanie responded with a soft clink of her own.

"Cheers," she echoed, and they drank, the cool liquid a mere footnote to the warmth growing between them as the lights dimmed once more.

The second act unfurled on stage, a tapestry of song and spectacle that held Melanie spellbound. But something new wove itself into her experience—an acute awareness of Lucas's gaze. It was tender and intense, like the touch of sun after a long winter, and it tugged at her concentration, making her heart flutter erratically.

She tried to immerse herself back into the fantastical world of Oz, but his presence was a constant pull. Every time Elphaba soared in defiant glory, Melanie felt Lucas's eyes not just on her, but through her, seeing parts of her she hadn't known were visible. She could feel the corners of her lips curling up involuntarily, responding to an unspoken dialogue between them.

With a final, rousing number, the show reached its crescendo and then bowed out to thunderous applause. Melanie joined in enthusiastically, but as the curtain fell for the last time, she turned to Lucas, her eyes bright with gratitude and excitement.

"Thank you," she said, her voice brimming with sincerity. "This—everything—it's been magical."

Lucas's smile deepened, creating soft crinkles around his eyes. "It was my pleasure. I'm glad to see you so happy."

They stepped out into the cool Portland night, the city alive around them. Hailing a taxi with practiced ease, Lucas held the door open for her before sliding in beside her. As the cab wove through the streets, they were cocooned in their own little world, discussing the layers of Elphaba's character.

"She's not wicked, she's misunderstood, and so complex," Melanie mused passionately. "That's what makes her so compelling."

"Exactly," Lucas agreed, watching her animated face with fascination. "It takes seeing things from a different angle to understand the whole picture."

As they continued to dissect the nuances of the show, the connection between them grew beyond the shared experience. It was in the way her laughter filled the spaces between his words, and how his insights prompted her to think deeper. The taxi ride back to the hotel was short, but the distance they traversed together was immeasurable, bridging gaps and weaving them closer with every passing moment.

The hotel room door clicked shut behind them, sealing off the buzz of nightlife. Melanie's gaze was immediately drawn to the bed where a silver tray adorned with chocolate-covered strawberries and two flutes of bubbling Sprite awaited. A small card nestled among the treats bore Lucas's neat handwriting: "To more sweet moments."

"Lucas, this is lovely," she said, the corners of her eyes crinkling as she smiled.

He shrugged with a playful modesty that made his broad shoulders seem less imposing. "I thought we might enjoy a little something after the show."

Melanie picked up a strawberry by its green top, the rich chocolate coating glossy under the soft lighting. She held it out to him, and he leaned in, taking a bite, his eyes never leaving hers. A drop of chocolate lingered at the corner of his mouth, and she reached out instinctively, thumb brushing against his skin to wipe it away. Her touch sparked a warm silence between them, filled only by the faint fizz of Sprite.

"Your turn," Lucas said, plucking a strawberry from the tray and holding it before her lips. As she bit into the sweet fruit, the taste mingled with the essence of the moment—indulgent, tender, and just a bit playful. They continued back and forth, feeding each other with gentle teases and soft laughter echoing in the room.

Sipping on the Sprite, the bubbles tickled Melanie's nose, causing her to giggle. The sound was bright and unrestrained, and she reveled in the freedom she felt with Lucas. It was as though the layers of reservation and caution built over the years were peeling away, petal by petal, under his attentive gaze.

"Who knew chocolate could be so intoxicating?" Melanie mused, leaning back against the plush pillows.

"Perhaps it's not the chocolate," Lucas replied, his voice low and infused with a hint of suggestion.

Melanie met his gaze, her heart fluttering like the wings of a captive bird finally set free. In that shared glance, words became unnecessary, and the room seemed to shrink to the space they occupied—their laughter, the soft pop of Sprite, and the chocolate sweetness lingering on their tongues crafting a world all their own.

Chapter Ten

The wheels of the plane touched down on the tarmac, a gentle rumble marking their return to Missouri. Melanie peered through the oval window, her playful grin from moments ago dissolving into a straight line as the familiar landscape ushered in a shift from weekend whimsy to workweek wariness.

"Back to reality, huh?" Lucas asked, noting the change in her demeanor.

"Seems like it," Melanie replied, her voice tinged with a mix of reluctance and resolve.

They exited the plane, a bustling St. Louis airport swallowing them whole. As they made their way through the terminal, Melanie's mind was already ticking through a checklist of tasks awaiting her attention. The fun of the weekend felt like a distant memory, one that she packed away along with her carry-on luggage.

They reached the car, a silver SUV that seemed to glint under the airport lights. No sooner had Melanie buckled her seatbelt than her phone chimed, a reminder of the world that didn't pause for leisurely getaways. Without hesitation, she answered, her voice all business.

"Hey, Abigail. Fill me in on how things went this weekend."

As Lucas started the engine and steered them onto the road home, Melanie listened intently to Abigail's report, nodding along to the updates and instructions.

"Okay, good. And the new batch of freeze-dried berries? Excellent. I'll check the inventory first thing tomorrow."

Melanie's words were crisp and efficient, every syllable painting the picture of a woman who ran not just a farm but a burgeoning enterprise. Lucas admired her dedication and the keen intellect that drove her success. He understood that the same ambition that drew him to her also meant sharing her with a constant stream of obligations and decisions.

"Make sure Jacob follows up with the suppliers," Melanie continued, her gaze now fixed on the road ahead.

Lucas watched her, the way her fingers danced across the screen, the furrow of concentration between her brows. He took in the view for just a moment longer before he acted.

"Melanie," he said gently but with enough command to slice through her focus. As she wrapped up her conversation with a curt nod, Lucas reached out and smoothly plucked the phone from her hands, his fingers brushing against the warmth of her skin.

"Hey!" Melanie's voice spiked with surprise, her eyes snapping to meet his, their green depths reflecting a mix of emotions—shock being the most prominent.

"Relax," he replied, offering her a grin that edged on playful mischief. "We still have until Monday morning before our weekend is over."

Her expression softened, and a laugh bubbled up from deep within.

"Lucas Barnett, you're a brat," she said, her laughter tapering off into a warm smile that crinkled the corners of her eyes.

"Only with you." His voice carried the weight of truth, laced with the hope of what their life together in Missouri could be—a blend of love, laughter, and shared dreams.

The neon sign of a cozy roadside diner flickered warmly against the gathering dusk as Melanie and Lucas pulled off the highway. The weariness from the flight had started to seep into Melanie's bones, but it was quickly dispelled as they stepped inside. The diner was a time capsule, with red vinyl booths and the aroma of coffee mingling with the scent of home-style cooking.

They slid into a booth by the window, and without a word, Lucas reached across the table, his fingers finding hers in a comforting grip.

"Remember this," he said, giving her hand a gentle squeeze. "Even when we're swamped with work, I'm still this guy holding your hand."

"I'll hold you to that," she replied, returning the pressure of his hand.

Their meal was relaxed and enjoyable, and Melanie realized he was right. Work could wait until morning, and she could just enjoy being with her husband.

"You're right. You have my complete attention until it's time for work tomorrow."

He grinned. "I ask for nothing in life more than that."

She laughed. "Oh, I'm certain you'll ask for more someday, but for now, it's enough."

THE WORLD DIDN'T SLOW its pace even a little in the week that followed. Each day was a whirlwind of activity, with Melanie orchestrating operations at the plant and Lucas splitting his time between the farm and the offices in the plant. Their hours were long, and the amount of time they had together seemed to dwindle daily.

Friday night arrived, cloaked in exhaustion and the smell of something new wafting from the kitchen. Melanie had decided to surprise Lucas with a new recipe she'd concocted with Abigail.

"Ready for a taste adventure?" she asked, setting down the plates .

"Always," Lucas replied, his eyes bright with anticipation. He took a bite, the layers of spices and textures playing across his palate. "This is incredible, Mel. You've outdone yourself."

"Thank you." She watched him with a mixture of pride and affection. "But?"

"But," he continued, his voice carrying a note of determination, "we need to talk about making some changes."

"Changes?" Melanie's fork paused mid-air, curiosity piqued.

"Nothing bad, I promise." Lucas reached across the table, his touch grounding. "I just think we could use a bit more balance. More nights like this, where it's just us, good food, and no talk of work."

Melanie considered his words, the businesswoman within her calculating the logistics. Yet, the woman who had laughed so freely in his car on the way back from Portland understood the value of what he proposed. A balanced life—one where love and ambition could flourish side by side.

"Balance is good," she conceded.

"Great," Lucas smiled, relief evident in his expression. "Because there's a puzzle waiting for us in the living room, and I plan on winning this time."

"Winning, huh?" Melanie chuckled, feeling the weight of the week lift from her shoulders. "We'll see about that, Mr. Barnett."

They cleared the table together before he showed her a puzzle he'd ordered from Amazon. As they settled down with the puzzle pieces scattered before them, Melanie felt their relationship was on the precipice of something. She only wished she knew what.

Melanie watched Lucas as he fiddled with the last piece of the puzzle, his brow furrowed in mock concentration. He turned to her, flashing a boyish grin.

"Mel," he said, taking a deep breath, "I've been thinking about something."

"Uh-oh," she teased, leaning against the kitchen counter, her arms folded. "Should I be worried?"

"Only if the idea of having more weekends like this worries you," he replied, crossing the room to stand beside her. His hand found hers, fingers intertwining naturally. "I want us to alternate being on call with Abigail and Jacob. I think we need that space, time for us to grow."

The words hung in the air between them, a proposal that challenged Melanie's deeply ingrained work ethic. Her mind raced through schedules, client needs, and productivity charts. To step back was to lose control, yet the warmth from his touch spoke of different possibilities.

"Lucas, you know the plant is my baby," Melanie said, her voice a blend of caution and intrigue. "Being away from work...it's not something I'm used to."

"I know," he acknowledged with a nod. "But I'm not talking about stepping back entirely. Just every other weekend. It's about finding a rhythm where work doesn't consume all our time. We need moments where it's just you and me, away from the daily grind."

She considered his words and thought about the wonderful time they'd had on their weekend away. A part of her resisted the change and feared the unknown that came with it. But then there was Lucas with his eyes filled with an earnest plea for shared moments, for laughter unburdened by deadlines.

"Extra time with you does sound tempting," she admitted, a smile tugging at the corners of her mouth. The thought of lingering mornings, unhurried conversations, and leisurely walks with him sparked a happiness she couldn't deny.

"Think about the puzzles we could conquer," he said, pulling her closer.

"Or the recipes I could botch without the threat of a phone call interrupting," she added playfully, resting her head against his chest.

"Exactly," he said, kissing the top of her head. "Life isn't just about the work we do. It's also about these moments. With you, Melanie, every moment counts."

Melanie felt a surge of hopefulness. She saw the promise of weekends spent having fun with him. Maybe there *was* more to life than just work.

"Okay," she said, her voice threading through the space between them like a delicate promise. "Every other weekend on call with Abigail and Jacob sounds like a perfect compromise."

"Perfect," he said, his lips curling into a smile.

AFTER SUPPER THE FOLLOWING evening, they cleared the dining table, making room for their fun project—a thousand-piece puzzle of the New York City skyline.

Lucas sat across from her, his long legs stretched out beneath the table, eyes tracing the constellations of freckles on Melanie's focused face. She bit her lip, a habit he'd learned signaled her deep concentration, as she turned pieces this way and that, searching for the right fit.

"Remember when you said you loved these puzzles because they reminded you of farming?" he asked, picking up a piece that appeared to be part of the Empire State Building.

"Of the land," she corrected without looking up. "How every little bit matters, how everything has its place. It's satisfying, seeing it all come together."

"Like us," Lucas mused aloud.

"Like us," she agreed, finally raising her eyes to meet his gaze.

The hours slipped by unnoticed as they worked side by side, laughter mingling with soft sighs of achievement whenever two pieces clicked together. Lucas thought it was liberating, sitting with Melanie, allowing himself to be lost in the pure joy of her company.

He leaned back in his chair, stretching his arms above his head, never taking his eyes off her. The way she chewed her lip, the furrow of her brow smoothing out as she found another match—it was these simple, ordinary moments that somehow felt extraordinary with her. And it dawned on him, somewhere between the clicking of puzzle pieces and her soft laughter, that he was completely in love with her.

It was not a lightning bolt or a thunderous revelation, but a gentle wave washing over him, leaving everything more vivid in its wake. He hadn't realized how much he'd been holding his breath until now, and as he exhaled, a sense of peace settled over him.

"Got another piece," Melanie announced triumphantly.

"Good job," he said, his voice soft with affection. "You're amazing, you know that?"

"Only at puzzles," she replied, her smile lighting up the room.

"No, at everything."

Melanie reached for another puzzle piece, her slender fingers brushing against Lucas's as she did. He hadn't moved his gaze from her, and she felt the weight of his stare with a mix of curiosity and a fluttering warmth in her chest. "What is it?" she asked, turning to catch his eye.

Lucas took a deep breath, the air seemingly charged with something new, something significant. "I love you," he said.

For a moment, Melanie froze, her heart skipping a beat. Then, the edges of her mouth curled into a smile that seemed to spread through her entire being. "I love you too," she replied, her voice a whisper. In an instant, the space between them vanished as she shifted closer, her hands finding his shoulders, pulling herself into his warm embrace.

Their lips met in a kiss that started gentle but grew in hunger and need. Melanie ended up on Lucas's lap, her arms wrapped around his neck, kissing him with a fervor that erased any remaining doubt of their connection.

They moved together, rising from the table cluttered with puzzle pieces toward the bedroom, their sanctuary. As they crossed the threshold, Melanie knew with unshakeable certainty that marrying Lucas was the right decision. Not just for her heart, which already knew its answer, but for her business, her future, her very self.

Melanie surrendered to the love she felt for Lucas, to the partnership they were building, and to the life they were creating together—one weekend, one puzzle piece at a time.

Epilogue

Months later, when it was time for planting again, Melanie sat with Lucas on the front porch swing of their modest farmhouse.

Lucas couldn't help but admire how she seemed so at ease here, this formidable woman who had turned her grandmother's legacy into a thriving enterprise. Her hands, always in motion during the daylight hours—whether tending to plants or crafting new recipes—were now still, resting on her lap.

He reached over, his calloused fingers finding hers and gently took her hand. "Beautiful, isn't it?" he said, gesturing toward the sunset with his free hand.

Melanie turned her head to meet his gaze. "Very," she agreed.

"Thank you," he whispered.

She looked at him with a question in her eyes, but then she understood. He was thanking her for all the days and weeks and months and years they would have together. "And thank you."

As the twilight deepened, Melanie's hand tightened slightly around his. There was a pause, a breath of time where anticipation hung between them, as tangible as the cool air that edged out the day's warmth.

"I need to tell you something important." Her gaze never wavered, though there was a flicker of something new. "I'm going to need you to step in more with the farm. To take over some of my duties for a while." She paused, then added in a voice barely above a whisper, "Because I'm pregnant, Lucas."

The words settled between them, weighty and wondrous. Lucas felt as if the world had shifted on its axis, his mind grappling with the magnitude of what she had revealed. Pregnant. They were going to have a child.

He looked at Melanie, really looked at her, seeing not only the woman who had captured his heart and ignited his soul but also the mother she would become. "Melanie," he said, his voice thick with emotion, "there's nothing I want more than to be there for you, for our baby. Whatever you need, I'm here."

Melanie smiled, leaning her head against his shoulder.

"Imagine," he said, "tiny feet running through these fields, laughter filling the air. Our child will grow up surrounded by all of this life, all of this love."

"Your excitement is the most beautiful thing I've seen." Melanie's eyes shimmered with unshed tears. Her gaze met his, steady and sure. "I can't wait to see you teach them about the world, to watch you hold them for the first time."

"Let's go inside," Melanie suggested, her voice brimming with anticipation. "We have so much to plan, so much to dream about."

"Lead the way," Lucas replied, his hand finding hers. They stepped through the threshold of their home. And in that evening, filled with simple rejoicing and profound love, Lucas and Melanie found themselves not just planning a life together but truly living it.